"ONE OF THE GREAT MAKERS
OF SCIENCE FICTION"
Jack Williamson

"Daniel Frost," said the judge, "I'll make this brief and to the point."

"You have been seized and brought to this court and have undergone a narco-trial. You have been found guilty of the charge and sentence already has been passed and executed."

"But that's ridiculous," Frost cried out. "What have I done? What was the charge?"

"Treason," said the judge.

"Treason. Your Honor, you are crazy. How could I . . ."

"Not treason to the state. Treason to humanity."

Frost stood rigid, his hands gripping the wood of the chair so hard that the grasp was painful. A tumult of fear went surging through him.

"It is the sentence of this court, in accordance with the penalty set out by the statutes, that you, Daniel Frost, shall be ostracized from the human race."

Why Call Them Back From Heaven?

CLIFFORD D. SIMAK

AVON
PUBLISHERS OF BARD, CAMELOT AND DISCUS BOOKS

AVON BOOKS
A division of
The Hearst Corporation
959 Eighth Avenue
New York, New York 10019

Copyright © 1967 by Clifford D. Simak
Published by arrangement with Doubleday & Company, Inc.
Library of Congress Catalog Card Number: 67-10392
ISBN: 0-380-50575-4

First Avon Printing, June, 1980

AVON TRADEMARK REG. U.S. PAT. OFF. AND IN
OTHER COUNTRIES, MARCA REGISTRADA,
HECHO EN U.S.A.

Printed in the U.S.A.

Why Call Them
Back From Heaven?

1

THE JURY chortled happily. The type bars blurred with frantic speed as they set down the Verdict, snaking smoothly across the roll of paper.

Then the Verdict ended and the judge nodded to the clerk, who stepped up to the Jury and tore off the Verdict. He held it ritually in two hands and turned toward the judge.

"The defendant," said the judge, "will rise and face the Jury."

Franklin Chapman rose shakily to his feet and Ann Harrison rose as well and stood beside him. She reached out a hand and laid it on his arm. Through the fabric of his shirt she felt the quiver of his flesh.

I should have done a better job, she told herself. Although, in all fact, she knew, she had worked harder on this case than she had on many others. Her heart had gone out to this man beside her, so pitiful and trapped. Perhaps, she thought, a woman had no right to defend a man in a court like this. In the ancient days, when the Jury had been human, it might have been all right. But not in a court where a computer was the Jury and the only point at issue was the meaning of the law.

"The clerk," said the judge, "now will read the Verdict."

She glanced at the prosecutor, sitting at his table, his face as stern and pontifical as it had been throughout the trial. An instrument, she thought—just an instrument, as the Jury was an instrument of justice.

The room was quiet and somber, with the sun of late afternoon shining through the windows. The newsmen sat in the front row seats, watching for the slightest flicker of emotion, for the tiny gesture of significance, for the slightest crumb upon which to build a story. The cameras were there as well, their staring lenses set to record this moment when eternity and nothingness quavered in the balance.

Although, Ann knew, there could be little doubt. There had been so little upon which to build a case. The Verdict would be death.

The clerk began to read:

"In the case of the State versus Franklin Chapman, the finding is that the said Chapman, the defendant in this action, did, through criminal negligence and gross lack of responsibility, so delay the recovery of the corpse of one Amanda Hackett as to make impossible the preservation of her body, resulting in conclusive death to her total detriment.

"The contention of the defendant that he, personally, was not responsible for the operating efficiency and the mechanical condition of the vehicle employed in the attempt to retrieve the body of the said Amanda Hackett, is impertinent to this action. His total responsibility encompassed the retrieval of the body by all and every means and to this over-all responsibility no limitations are attached. There may be others who will be called upon to answer to this matter of irresponsibility, but the measure of their innocence or guilt can have no bearing upon the issue now before the court.

"The defendant is judged guilty upon each and every count. In lack of extenuating circumstances, no recommendation for mercy can be made."

Chapman sank slowly down into his chair and sat there, straight and stiff, his great mechanic's hands clasped tightly together on the table, his face a frozen slab.

All along, Ann Harrison told herself, he had known how it would be. That was why he was taking it so well. He had not been fooled a minute by her lawyer talk or by her assurances. She had tried to hold him together and she need not have bothered, for all along he'd known how it was and he'd made his bargain with himself and now he was keeping it.

"Would defense counsel," asked the judge, "care to make a motion?"

Said Ann, "If Your Honor pleases."

He is a good man, Ann told herself. He's trying to be kind, but he can't be kind. The law won't let him be. He'll listen to my motion and he will deny it and then pronounce the sentence and that will be the end of it. For there was nothing more that anyone could do. In the light of evidence, no appeal was possible.

She glanced at the waiting newsmen, at the scanning television eyes, and felt a little tremor of panic running in her veins. Was it wise, she asked herself, this move that she had planned? Futile, certainly; she knew that it was futile. But aside from its futility, how about the wisdom of it?

And in that instant of her hesitation, she knew that she had to do it, that it lay within the meaning of her duty and she could not fail that duty.

"Your Honor," she said, "I move that the Verdict be set aside on the grounds of prejudice."

The prosecutor bounded to his feet.

His Honor waved him back into his chair.

"Miss Harrison," said the judge, "I am not certain that I catch your meaning. Upon what grounds do you mention prejudice?"

She walked around the table so that she might better face the judge.

"On the grounds," she said, "that the key evidence concerned mechanical failure of the vehicle the defendant used in his official duties."

The judge nodded gravely. "I agree with you. But how can the character of the evidence involve prejudice?"

"Your Honor," said Ann Harrison, "the Jury also is mechanical."

The prosecutor was on his feet again.

"Your Honor!" he brayed. "Your Honor!"

The judge banged his gavel.

"I can take care of this," he told the prosecutor, sternly.

The newsmen were astir, making notes, whispering among themselves. The television lenses seemed to shine more brightly.

The prosecutor sat down. The buzz subsided. The room took on a deadly quiet.

"Miss Harrison," asked the judge, "you challenge the objectivity of the Jury?"

"Yes, Your Honor. Where machines may be involved. I do not claim it is a conscious prejudice, but I do claim that unconscious prejudice ..."

9

"Ridiculous!" said the prosecutor loudly.

The judge shook his gavel at him.

"You be quiet," he said.

"But I do claim," said Ann, "that a subconscious prejudice could be involved. And I further contend that in any mechanical contrivance there is one lacking quality essential to all justice—the sense of mercy and of human worth. There is law, I'll grant you, a superhuman, total knowledge of the law, but . . ."

"Miss Harrison," said the judge, "you're lecturing the court."

"I beg Your Honor's pardon."

"You are finished, then?"

"I believe I am, Your Honor."

"All right, then. I'll deny this motion. Have you any others?"

"No, Your Honor."

She went around the table, but did not sit down.

"In that case," said the judge, "there is no need to delay the sentence. Nor have I any latitude. The law in cases such as this is expressly specific. The defendant will stand."

Slowly Chapman got to his feet.

"Franklin Chapman," said the judge, "it is the determination of this court that you, by your conviction of these charges and in the absence of any recommendation for mercy, shall forfeit the preservation of your body at the time of death. Your civil rights, however, are in no other way impaired."

He banged his gavel.

"This case is closed," he said.

2

DURING the night someone had scrawled a slogan on the wall of a dirty red brick building that stood across the street. The heavy yellow chalk marks read:

WHY CALL THEM BACK FROM HEAVEN?

Daniel Frost wheeled his tiny two-place car into its space in one of the parking lots outside Forever Center and got out, standing for a moment to stare at the sign.

There had been a lot of them recently, chalked here and everywhere, and he wondered, a little idly, what was going on that would bring about such a rash of them. Undoubtedly Marcus Appleton could tell him if he asked about it, but Appleton, as security chief of Forever Center, was a busy man and in the last few weeks Frost had seen him, to speak to, only once or twice. But if there were anything unusual going on, he was sure that Marcus would be on top of it. There wasn't much, he comforted himself, that Marcus didn't know about.

The parking lot attendant walked up and touched his cap by way of greeting.

"Good morning, Mr. Frost. Looks like heavy traffic."

And indeed it did. The traffic lanes were filled, bumper to bumper, with tiny cars almost identical with the one that Frost had parked. Their plastic bubble domes glinted in the morning sun and from where he stood he could catch the faint electric whining of the many motors.

"The traffic's always heavy," he declared. "And that reminds me. You better take a look at my right-hand buffer. Another car came too close for comfort."

"Might have been the other fellow's buffer," the attendant

11

said, "but it won't hurt to check on it. And what about the padding, Mr. Frost? It can freeze up, you know."

"I think it's all right," said Frost.

"I'll check it anyhow. Won't take any time. No sense in taking chances."

"I suppose you're right," said Frost. "And thank you, Tom."

"We have to work together," the attendant told him. "Watch out for one another. That slogan means a lot to me. I suppose someone in your department wrote it."

"That is right," said Frost. "Some time ago. It is one of our better efforts. A participation motto."

He reached inside the car and took the briefcase off the seat, tucked it underneath his arm. The package of lunch that he carried in it made an untidy bulge.

He stepped onto the elevated safety walk and headed along it toward one of the several plazas built all around the towering structure of Forever Center. And now, as he always did, and for no particular reason that he could figure out, he threw back his head and stared up at the mile-high wall of the mighty building. There were times, on stormy mornings, when the view was cut off by the clouds that swirled about its top, but on a clear morning such as this the great slab of masonry went up and up until its topmost stories were lost in the blue haze of the sky. A man grew dizzy looking at it and the mind reeled at the thought of what the hand of man had raised.

He stumbled and only caught himself in the nick of time. He'd have to stop this crazy staring upward at the building, he told himself, or, at least, wait to do it until he reached the plaza. The safety walk was only two feet high, but a man could take a nasty tumble if he didn't watch himself. It was not impossible that he might break his neck. He wondered, for the hundredth time, why someone didn't think to protect the walks with railings.

He reached the plaza and let himself down off the safety walk into the jam-packed crowd that struggled toward the building. He hugged the briefcase tight against him and tried, with one hand, to protect the bulge that was his sack of lunch. Although, he knew, there was little chance of protecting it. Almost every day it was crushed by the pack of bodies that filled the plaza and the lobby of the building.

Perhaps, he thought, he should go without the usual milk today. He could get a cup of water when he ate his lunch and it would do as well. He licked his lips, which suddenly were dry. Maybe, he told himself, there was some other way he might save the extra money. For he did like that daily glass of milk and looked forward to it with a great deal of pleasure.

There was no question about it, however. He'd have to find a way to make up for the cost of energizing the buffer on the car. It was an expense he had not counted on and it upset his budget. And if Tom should find that some of the padding would have to be replaced, that would mean more money down the drain.

He groaned a bit, internally, as he thought about it.

Although, he realized, a man could not take any sort of chances—not with all the drivers on the road.

No chances—no chances of any kind that would threaten human life. No more daredeviltry, no more mountain climbing, no more air travel, except for the almost foolproof helicopter used in rescue work, no more auto racing, no more of the savage contact sports. Transportation made as safe as it could be made, elevators equipped with fantastic safety features, stairways safeguarded with non-skid treads and the steps themselves of resilient material . . . everything that could be done being done to rule out accident and protect human life. Even the very air, he thought, protected from pollution—fumes from factories filtered and recycled to extract all irritants, cars no longer burning fossil fuels but operating on almost everlasting batteries that drove electric motors.

A man had to live, this first life, as long as he was able. It was the only opportunity that he had to lay away a competence for his second life. And when every effort of the society in which he lived was bent toward the end of the prolongation of his life, it would never do to let a piece of carelessness or an exaggerated sense of economy (such as flinching at the cost of a piece of padding or the re-energizing of a buffer) rob him of the years needed to tuck away the capital he would need in the life to come.

He remembered, as he inched along, that this was conference morning and that he'd have to waste an hour or more listening to B.J. sound off about a lot of things that

13

everyone must know. And when B.J. was through, the heads of the various departments and project groups would bring up problems which they could solve without any help, but bringing them up as an excuse to demonstrate how busy and devoted and how smart they were. It was a waste of time, Frost told himself, but there was no way to get out of it. Every week for several years, ever since he had become head of the public relations department, he had trooped in with the rest of them and sat down at the conference table, fidgeting when he thought of the work piled on his desk.

Marcus Appleton, he thought, was the only one of them who had any guts. Marcus refused to attend the conferences and he got away with it. Although, perhaps, he was the only one who could. Security was a somewhat different proposition than the other departments. If security was to be effective, it had to have a somewhat freer hand than was granted any of the other people of Forever Center.

There had been times, he recalled, when he had been tempted to lay some of his problems on the table for consideration at the meetings. But he never had and now was glad he hadn't. For any of the contributions and suggestions made would have been entirely worthless. Although that would not have prevented people from other departments claiming credit, later, for any effective work that he had been able to turn out.

The thing to do, he told himself, as he had many times before, was to do his work, keep his mouth shut and lay away every penny that he could lay his hands upon.

Thinking about his work, he wondered who had thought up the slogan chalked on the red brick wall. It was the first time he had seen it and it was the most effective one so far and he could use the man who had dreamed it up. But it would be a waste of time, he knew, to try to find the man and offer him the job. The slogan undoubtedly was Holies work and all the Holies were a stiff-necked bunch.

Although what they hoped to gain by their opposition to Forever Center was more than he could figure. For Forever Center was not aimed against religion, nor against one's faith. It was no more than a purely scientific approach to a biological program of far-reaching consequence.

He struggled up the stairs to the entrance, sliding and inching his way along, and came into the lobby. Bearing to

14

the right, he slid along, foot by foot, to reach the hobby stand that was flanked on one side by the tobacco counter and on the other by the drug concession.

The space in front of the drug counter was packed. People stopping on their way to work to pick up their dream pills—hallucinatory drugs—that would give them a few pleasant hours come evening. Frost had never used them, never intended to—for they were, he thought, a foolish waste of money, and he had never felt that he really needed them.

Although, he supposed, there were those who felt they needed them—something to make up for what they felt they might be missing, the excitement and adventure of those former days when man walked hand in hand with a death that was an utter ending. They thought, perhaps, that the present life was a drab affair, that it had no color in it, and that the purpose they must hold to was a grinding and re-morseless purpose. There would be such people, certainly—the ones who would forget at times the breath-taking glory of this purpose in their first life, losing momentary sight of the fact that this life they lived was no more than a few years of preparation for all eternity.

He worked his way through the crowd and reached the hobby stand, which was doing little business.

Charley, the owner of the stand, was behind the counter, and as he saw Frost approaching, reached down into the case and brought out a stock card on which a group of stamps were ranged.

"Good morning, Mr. Frost," he said. "I have something here for you. I saved it special for you."

"Swiss again, I see," said Frost.

"Excellent stamps," said Charley. "I'm glad to see you buying them. A hundred years from now you'll be glad you did. Good solid issues put out by a country in the blue chips bracket."

Frost glanced down at the lower right-hand corner of the card. A figure, 1.30, was written there in pencil.

"The price today," said Charley, "is a dollar, eighty-five."

3

THE wind had blown down the cross again, sometime in the night.

The trouble, thought Ogden Russell, sitting up and rubbing his eyes to rid them of the seeping pus that had hardened while he slept, was that sand was a poor thing in which to set a cross. Perhaps, if he could find them, several sizable boulders placed around its base might serve to hold it upright against the river breeze.

He'd have to do something about it, for it was not meet nor proper that the cross, poor thing that it might be, should topple with every passing gust. It was not, he told himself, consistent with his piety and purpose.

He wondered, sitting there upon the sand, with the morning laughter of the river in his ears, if he had been as wise as he had thought in picking out this tiny island as his place of solitude. It had solitude, all right, but it had little else. The one thing that it lacked, quite noticeably, was comfort. Although comfort, he reminded himself quite sternly, had been a quality that he had not sought. There had been comfort back where he had come from, in that world he'd turned his back upon, and he could have kept it by simply staying there. But he had forsaken comfort, and many other things as well, in this greater search for something which he could sense and feel but which, as yet, he had not come to grips with.

Although I've tried, he thought. My God, how I have tried!

He arose and stretched, carefully and gingerly, for he had, it seemed, an ache in every bone and a soreness in each muscle. It's this sleeping out, he thought, that does it, exposed to the wind and to the river damp, without so much as a ragged blanket to drape his huddled self. With

16

almost nothing to cover him, in fact, for the only thing he wore was an ancient pair of trousers, chopped above the knees.

Having stretched, he wondered if he should set up the cross before his morning prayer, or if the prayer might be as acceptable without a standing cross. After all, he told himself, there would be a cross, a reclining cross, and surely the validity lay in the symbol of the cross itself and not its attitude.

Standing there, he wrestled with his conscience and tried to look into his soul and into the immutable mystery of that area which stretched beyond his soul, and which still remained elusive of any understanding. And there was still no insight and there was no answer, as there had never been an answer. It was worse this morning than it had ever been. For all that he could think of was the peeling sunburn of his body, the abrasions of his knees from kneeling in the sand, the knot of hunger in his belly, and the wondering about whether there might be a catfish on one of the lines he'd set out the night before.

If there were no answer yet, he told himself, after months of waiting, of seeking for that answer, perhaps it was because there was no answer and this had been a senseless course upon which he'd set himself. He might be pounding at the door of an empty room; might be calling upon a thing which did not exist and never had existed, or calling upon it by a name it did not recognize.

Although, he thought, the name would be of no consequence. The name was simply form, no more than a framework within which a man might operate. Really, he reminded himself, the thing he hunted was a simple thing—an understanding and a faith, the depth of faith and the strength of understanding that men of old had held. There must, he argued, be some basis for the belief that it existed somewhere and that it could be found. Mankind, as a whole, could not be so completely wrong. Religious faith, of any sort, must be something more than a mere device of man's own making to fill the aching void that lay in mankind's heart. Even the old Neanderthalers had laid their dead so that when they rose to second life they would face the rising sun, and had sprinkled in the grave the handsful of red ocher symbolic of that second life, and had left with

17

the dead those weapons and adornments they would need in the life to come.

And he had to know! He must force himself to know! And he would know, when he had schooled himself to reach deep into the hidden nature of existence. Somewhere in that mystic pool he would find the truth.

There must be more to life, he thought, than continued existence on this earth, no matter for how long. There must be another eternity somewhere beyond the reawakened and renewed and immortal flesh.

Today, this very day, he'd rededicate himself. He'd spend a longer time upon his knees and he'd seek the deeper and he'd shut out all else but the search he had embarked upon —and this might be the day. Somewhere in the future lay the hour and minute of his understanding and his faith and there was no telling when that hour might strike. It might, indeed, be close.

For this he'd need all his strength and he'd have his breakfast first, even before the morning prayer, and thus reinforced, he'd enter once again with a renewed vigor upon his seeking after truth.

He went along the sandspit to the willows where he had tied his lines and he pulled them in. They came in easily and there was nothing on them.

The hard ball of hunger squeezed the tighter as he stared at the empty hooks.

So it would be river clams again. He gagged at the thought of them.

4

B.J. RAPPED sharply on the table with a pencil to signal the beginning of the meeting. He looked benevolently around at the people there.

"I am glad to see you with us, Marcus," said B.J. "You don't often make it. I understand you have a little problem."

Marcus Appleton glowered back at B.J.'s benevolence. "Yes, B.J.," he said, "there is a little problem, but not entirely mine."

B.J. swung his gaze on Frost. "How's the new thrift campaign coming, Dan?"

Frost said, "We are working on it."

"We're counting on you," B.J. told him. "It has to have some punch in it. I hear a lot of investment cash is going into stamps and coins. . . ."

"The trouble is," said Frost, "that stamps and coins are a good long-range investment."

Peter Lane, treasurer, stirred uncomfortably in his chair. "The quicker you can come up with something," he said, "the better it will be. Subscriptions to our stock have been falling off quite noticeably." He looked around the table. "Stamps and coins!" he said, as if they were dirty words.

"We could put a stop to it," said Marcus Appleton. "All we need to do is drop a word or two. No more commemoratives, no more semi-postals, no more fancy air mail issues."

"You forget one thing," Frost reminded him. "It's not only stamps and coins. It's porcelain, as well, and paintings and a lot of other things. Almost anything that will fit into a time vault that is not too large. You can't put a stop to everything that is being bought."

19

CLIFFORD D. SIMAK

B.J. said, tartly, "We can't stop anything. There's already too much talk about how we own the world."

Carson Lewis, vice-president in charge of facilities, said, "I think it's talk of that kind which keeps the Holies active. Not, of course, that they're causing too much trouble, but they are a nuisance."

"There was a new sign across the street," said Lane. "A rather good one, I must say . . ."

"It's not there any more," Appleton said, between his teeth.

"No, I imagine not," said Lane. "But simply running around behind these people with a bucket and a brush and scrubbing off their signs is not the entire answer."

"I don't think," said Lewis, "there is any entire answer. The ideal thing, of course, would be to root out the entire Holies operation. But I doubt that's possible. Marcus, I think, will agree with me that all we can do is hold it down a little."

"It seems to me," said Lane, "that we could do more than we are doing. In the last few weeks I've seen more slogans chalked on walls than I've ever seen before. The Holies must have quite a corps of sign painters working surreptitiously. And it's not only here. It is everywhere. All up and down the coast. And in Chicago and in the West Coast complex. In Europe and in Africa . . ."

"Some day," said Appleton, "there'll be an end to it. I can promise that. There are just a few ringleaders. A hundred or so, perhaps. Once we have them pegged, we can put an end to it."

"But quietly, Marcus," B.J. cautioned. "I insist it must be quietly."

Appleton showed his teeth. "Very quiet," he said.

"It's not just the slogans," said Lewis. "There are the rumors, too."

"Rumors can't hurt us," B.J. said.

"Most of them can't, of course," said Lewis. "They're just something that give people something to talk about, to pass away the time. But there are some that have a basis of truth. And by that I mean that they are based on situations which do exist in Forever Center. They start with a truth and twist it in an ugly way and I think that some of those may hurt us. Rumors of any sort hurt our image. Some of them hurt us quite a lot. But the thing that worries me is how do these Holies learn of the situations upon which they base the rumors? I would suspect that they may have developed many pipelines into this very building and into other branches of Forever Center and that is something that we should try to put a stop to."

"We can't be sure," Lane protested, "that all the rumors are started by the Holies. I think we are inclined to attribute too much to them. They're just a gang of crackpots . . ."

"Not entirely crackpots," said Marcus Appleton. "We could clean out the crackpots. This bunch is a group of smart operators. The worst thing we can do is to underestimate them. My office is working on it all the time. We have a lot of information. I have a feeling that we may be closing in. . . ."

"I would agree with you," Lewis told him. "About their being an effective and well-organized opposition. I have often felt they might have some tie-up with the Loafers. Things get too hot, those who have the heat on them can simply disappear into the wilderness and hide out with the Loafers. . . ."

Appleton shook his head. "The Loafers are nothing more or less than they appear to be. You're letting your imagination run away with you, Carson. The Loafers are the unemployables, the chronic no-goods, the misfits. Comprising, what is it, Peter, something like one per cent . . ."

"Less than a half of one per cent," said Lane.

"All right, then, less than one half of one per cent of the population. They've declared themselves free of us, in effect. They roam the wilderness in bands. They scrape out a living somehow . . ."

"Gentlemen," said B.J. quietly, "I am afraid we're getting rather far afield into a subject we've discussed many times before, with no particular results. I would imagine we can leave the Holies to the close attention of Security."

Marcus nodded. "Thank you, B.J.," he said.

"Which brings us," said B.J., "to the problem that I mentioned."

Chauncey Hilton, section chief of the Timesearch project, spoke softly, "One of our research people has disappeared. Her name is Mona Campbell. I have a feeling that she was onto something."

"But if she was on the track of something," Lane exploded, "why should she . . ."

"Peter, please," said B.J. "Let's discuss this as calmly as we can."

He looked about the table. "I am sorry, gentlemen, that we did not let you know immediately. I suppose it wasn't something that we should have kept quiet about. But it was something that we didn't want noised around too much and Marcus thought . . ."

"Marcus has been looking for her, then?" asked Lane.

Appleton nodded. "Six days. There's been no trace of her."

"Maybe," Lewis said, "she just went off somewhere to be alone and think a problem through."

"We thought of that," said Hilton. "But if that had been the case, she would have spoken to me. A most conscientious person. And her notes are gone."

"If she'd gone off to work," insisted Lewis, "she'd have taken them along."

"Not all of them," said Hilton. "Just the current working notes. Not the entire file. Really, no one is supposed to take anything out of the project. Our security, however, is not as tight as it perhaps should be."

Lane said to Appleton, "You've checked the monitors?"

Appleton nodded, curtly. "Of course, we did. That's routine, for all the good it does us. The monitoring system is not set up to deal with identity. Each computer picks up a person when they show up in its quadrant, but it is simply concerned with the signal which establishes the fact there is a living person there. If one of the signals clicks off, then it knows someone has died and a rescue crew is dispatched at once. But these signals keep shifting all the time as people move about. They shift off one quadrant and are picked up by another."

"But it could indicate a person traveling."

"Certainly. But a lot of people travel. And Mona Campbell may have done no traveling. She may have just holed up."

"Or been kidnaped," Lewis said.

"I don't think so," Hilton told him. "You forget the notes are gone."

"You think, then," said Frost, "that she defected. Deliberately quit the project."

"She ran away," said Hilton.

Howard Barnes, head of Spacesearch, asked, "You really think she made some sort of breakthrough?"

"I think so," Hilton said. "She told me, rather guardedly, she was following a new line of calculation. I remember that distinctly. She said a new line of calculation rather than a new line of research. I thought it rather strange, but she had an intense look about her and . . ."

"She said calculation?" Lane asked.

"Yes. I found out later that she was working with the Hamal math. You remember it, Howard?"

Barnes nodded. "One of our ships brought it back—oh, say, twenty years ago. Found it on a planet that at one time had been occupied by an intelligent race. Probably a planet that we could use, but it would have to be terraformed and the terraforming on this particular planet would be a nasty job that might take a thousand years or more on an all-out effort."

"This math?" asked Lewis. "Anything we could use?"

"Mathematicians tried to figure it out," said Barnes. "Nothing came of it. It was recognizable as math, all right, but it was so far from our concept of math that no one could manage to get his teeth into it. The team that visited the planet found a lot of other artifacts, but the rest of them didn't seem to mean too much. Interesting, of course, to an anthropologist or to a culturist, but with no immediate practical value. The math, however, was something else again. It was in a—well, I suppose you could call it a book and the book seemed to be intact. It's not often you find any intact, spelled-out body of knowledge on an abandoned planet. There was quite a bit of excitement when it was brought home."

"And no one had cracked it," said Lane, "except possibly this Mona Campbell."

"I'm almost sure she did," said Hilton. "She is a rather exceptional person and . . ."

"You don't require periodic reports of work in progress?" asked Lane.

"Oh, yes, certainly. But we don't look over people's shoulders. You know what that can do."

"Yes," said Barnes. "They have to have some freedom. They have to be allowed to feel that a certain line of research belongs, personally, to them during its development."

B.J. said, "All of you, of course, realize how important this could be. With all respect to Howard, the Spacesearch program is a long-range project. It's something to look forward to three or four hundred years from now. But the time program we need as soon as we can get it. A breakthrough in the time program would assure us of the living space we will need, perhaps, in another century. Maybe before that. Once we begin revivals, we'll face a not too distant day when we'll need more space than this present earth affords. And the day we begin revivals may not be too distant. The Immortality boys are coming along quite nicely if I understand what Anson tells me rightly."

"That is right, B.J.," said Anson Graves. "We feel we are getting close. I'd say ten years at most."

"In ten years," said B.J., "we'll have immortality . . ."

"A lot could go wrong," warned Graves.

"We'll trust there won't," B.J. said. "In ten years we'll have immortality. The matter converters have solved the problem of materials and food. The housing program is up to schedule. All that we can look forward to as any massive problem is the matter of space. To get that space and get it quickly, we need time travel. Time is critical."

"Perhaps," suggested Lane, "we're looking for the impossible. Time may be something that can't be cracked. There may be nothing there."

"I can't agree with you," said Hilton. "I think Miss Campbell cracked it."

"And ran away," said Lane.

"It all boils down to one thing," said B.J. "Mona Campbell must be found."

He looked hard at Marcus Appleton. "You understand," he said. "Mona Campbell must be found!"

"I agree," said Appleton. "I would like to request, however, all the assistance that anyone can give me. In time, of course, we'll find her, but we might find her sooner if . . ."

"I don't quite understand," said Lane. "The matter of security is something that rests entirely in your hands."

"As a working proposition," said Appleton, "as an everyday affair, that is entirely true. But the treasury department also has its agents . . ."

"But for a different sort of work," exploded Lane. "Not for routine . . ."

"I agree with you," said Appleton, "although it is conceivable that they could be of help. There is one other department that I am thinking of."

He switched about in his chair and looked straight at Frost.

"Dan," he said, "you've developed a rather fine extracurricular intelligence that might be a lot of help. You have all sorts of tipsters and undercover boys and . . ."

"What is this?" B. J. demanded.

"Oh, I forgot," said Appleton. "You may not know about it. It's entirely a departmental affair. Dan has done a fine job in organizing this group of people and it's most effective. He finances it, I understand, out of something called publication research that doesn't necessarily come up for review. Which is true, of course, of a number of other activities and projects."

Why, you bastard, Frost said to himself. You dirty, lousy bastard!

"Dan," B.J. yelped, "is this the truth?"

"Yes," said Frost. "Yes, of course it is."

"But why?" demanded B.J. "Why should you have . . ."

"B.J.," said Frost, "if you are really interested I can cite you chapter and verse on why it's done and why it's necessary. Do you have any idea how many books, how many magazine articles, would have been published in the past year, or the past ten years—all of them purporting to expose Forever Center—if something hadn't been done to head them off?"

"No," yelled B.J. "And I'm not interested. We can survive those kind of attacks. We've survived them all before."

"We've survived them," said Frost, "because only a few slipped through. The worst of them were stopped. Not only by myself, but by the men who preceded me. There are some I've stopped that would have hurt us badly."

"B.J.," said Lane, "I think Dan has something on his side. I think that . . ."

"Well, I don't," B.J. stormed. "We shouldn't try to stop

anything, manage anything, censor anything. We are being accused of trying to run the world. It is being said . . ."

"B.J.," Frost said, angrily, "there is no use in our pretending that Forever Center doesn't run the earth. There are nations still, and governments, but we own the earth. We have soaked up all the investment capital and we own all the big enterprises and utilities and . . ."

"I could give you argument on that," roared B.J.

"Of course you could. It's not our capital. It's only money that we hold in trust. But we manage all that money and we decide how to invest it and no one can question us."

"I submit," said Lane, uneasily, "that we've wandered off the track."

"I hadn't meant," said Appleton, "to stir up a hornet's nest."

"I think you did," Frost told him levelly. "I don't know what the pitch is, Marcus, but you never did a thing in all your life that you didn't plan to do."

"Marcus, I believe, asked cooperation," said Lane, trying to calm the situation. "For my part, I'm willing to cooperate."

"For my part, I am not," said Frost. "I won't cooperate with a man who walked in here deliberately and tried to put me on the spot for doing a job that was being done long before I took over, and was conducted, as I've conducted it, in a decent secrecy . . ."

"I don't like it, Dan," B.J. told him.

"I knew you wouldn't like it," said Frost. "You are—you'll pardon the expression—our front man and I had no wish to embarrass you . . ."

"You knew?" B.J. asked of Lane.

Lane nodded. "Yes. The treasury had to supply the funds. And Marcus knew because he makes it his business to know everything. But there were just the three of us. I'm sorry, sir."

"I'll talk to the three of you about this later," said B.J. "I still am of the opinion that we should always operate openly and aboveboard. We hold a sacred trust. This organization has held that trust for a long, long time and we've held it in close honor. There will come a day when we will be called upon to make an accounting to all those people who are waiting for the day that we work toward. And when that day comes, I would hope we might be able to open, not only our books, but our hearts, for all the world to see. . . ."

B.J. was off on a topic that was dear to him. He could talk on it for hours.

He droned on and on.

Frost glanced at Appleton. The man was hunched tensely in his chair and scowling.

So it didn't work, thought Frost. Not the way you thought it would. You came in here primed and cocked and you let me have it and it didn't work entirely. And I wish I knew what was back of it, why you tried to get me.

For there had never been bad blood between himself and Marcus. Not that he'd been friendly with the man, for no man ever was a friend of Marcus Appleton. But they had been, if not friends, at least colleagues, each respectful of the other.

There must be something going on, he thought, something not apparent to the eye, some development somewhere that he had failed to catch. For if something were not going on, why had Appleton tried to ruin him?

He became conscious once again of B.J.'s words.

"And that is why, I say, we must bend all our resources to finding Mona Campbell. She may have something that we need, that we've needed all these years."

He stopped and looked inquiringly around the table. No one said a thing.

B.J. rapped on the table with his pencil.

"That is all," he said.

5

"You see, it's this way," said the little old lady to the mortician. "We both are getting old. It isn't as if we had a lot of years ahead of us. Although our health is good."

The old gentleman banged his cane upon the floor in glee and chuckled.

"That is the thing of it," he said. "Our health is just a bit too good. More than likely the both of us could go on living for another twenty years."

"And we enjoy it, too," the little old lady said. "James worked so hard all his life and we scrimped and saved. Now that he can't work any more, we have time just to sit and take it easy and do a little talking and go visiting and such. But we're going behind, financially, every blessed day. We are using up the little that we've saved and we can't have that."

"It's foolish," the old gentleman declared. "If we put ourselves away, the money that is left would go on earning interest."

The old lady nodded vigorously. "Earning interest," she said, "instead of us just sitting around and eating into it."

The mortician rubbed soft, flabby hands together.

"I quite understand," he said. "There is no need of you to feel embarrassment. People with your problem come in all the time."

6

FROM the window of his office, on the topmost floor of Forever Center, Frost stared out across the tapestry that was old New York. The Hudson was a strip of silver, shining in the morning sun, and the island of Manhattan was a patchwork of faded colors.

Many times before he had stood at this window and gazed out, seeing the scene below, framed by the blue haze of distance and of water, as a symbolic thing—a glimpse into the past of mankind from the vantage of the future.

But today the symbolism was not there. There was nothing but the nagging question and the worry that hammered at his brain.

There was no question but that Appleton had tried, deliberately, to put him on the spot, and while that, in itself, was frightening enough, the crux of the entire question was why Marcus had felt it necessary. Had it been Appleton alone, or had the man been acting for other interests, perhaps more involved?

Office politics—that would be the normal answer. But Frost, through the years, had studiously avoided involvement in office politics. Someone might want his job— perhaps many people did. But none of these, he was fairly certain, could engineer what Appleton had done.

And that left only one thing—that someone was afraid of him, that he knew something or suspected something that could be damaging, perhaps not to Forever Center, but to some of its department heads.

Which was ridiculous on the face of it. He did his job and minded his own business. He was consulted only on matters which touched upon his duties. He was not involved in policy other than whatever implementation of policy he was able to carry out promotionally.

He always had minded his own business, but this morning, he reminded himself, he'd stepped beyond the rule he had placed upon himself. He had told B.J. that it was ridiculous to pretend that Forever Center did not run the world. It was true enough, of course, but he should not have said it. He should have kept his mouth shut. There had been no need to say it. The one excuse he had was that he had been angered by Appleton and had acted in anger rather than in common sense.

What Appleton had said was the truth. There was a network of undercover people, but it was a system which had been handed on to him and it was small and restricted in its purpose. Appleton, for his own purposes, had blown it up far beyond the fact.

Frost turned from the window and went back to his desk. Sitting down, he reached out and pulled in front of him the stack of papers that Miss Beale had placed there. On top of the pile, as usual, was the daily report on vital statistics.

He picked it up and glanced at it.

There was simply the date, June 15, 2148, and then two lines of type:

In Abeyance—96,674,321,458

Viable—47,128,932,076

Scarcely glancing at the sheet, he crumpled it in his fist and dropped it in the wastebasket, then picked up the second paper off the stack.

There was a rustle at the door of the outer office and Frost looked up. Miss Beale stood there.

"I'm sorry, Mr. Frost," she said. "You weren't here, so I read the morning paper, then forgot to put it on your desk."

"It's quite all right," he said. "Anything of interest?"

"It has the release on the Cygnian expedition. They used it just the way we wrote it. You'll find it on page three."

"Not page one?" he asked.

"No. There was this Chapman case."

"Chapman case?"

"Yes, you know. The man whose rescue car broke down."

"Oh, that one. It's been in the news for days."

"He was sentenced yesterday. It was on TV."

"I missed it. I didn't turn on the set last night."

"It was so dramatic," said Miss Beale. "He has a wife

and children and now he can't go with them into second life. I feel so sorry for them."

"He broke the law," said Frost. "He failed a plain and simple duty. The lives of all of us depend on men like him."

"That is true," Miss Beale admitted, "but I still feel sad about it. Such a dreadful thing. To be only one out of many billions who is condemned to everlasting death, to miss the second chance."

"He is not the first one," Frost reminded her. "And he will not be the last."

She laid the paper on the corner of the desk.

"I heard," she said, "you had some trouble at this morning's meeting."

He nodded bleakly, saying nothing.

She had heard, he thought. Already the story of what had happened had been leaked somehow and now was racing like wildfire through the building.

"I hope it's not too bad," she said.

"It's not too bad," he told her.

She turned and started for the door.

"Miss Beale," he said.

She turned around.

"I'll be gone this afternoon," he told her. "There's nothing coming up, is there?"

"You have a couple of appointments. Not important. I can cancel them."

"If you would," he said.

"There may be a confidential file."

"Put it in the safe."

"But they don't like . . ."

"I know. It should be checked at once and . . ."

And that was it! he thought.

That was the answer to what Appleton had done.

It was simply something he had not thought about.

"Mr. Frost, is there something wrong?"

"No, not a thing. If a confidential file shows up, just put it in the safe. I'll tend to it, come morning."

"Very well," she said, a little stiffly to express her disapproval.

She swung about and went into the outer office.

He sat limply at his desk, remembering that day three months or so ago—when the messenger boy had somehow left, instead of his own confidential file, the one that should have gone to Peter Lane, and how he had opened it without looking at the name.

He had taken it back, personally, and explained to Lane and it had seemed to be all right. The messenger boy had been fired, of course, but that was all that happened. It had been a mistake, a grave mistake, on the part of the messenger, and he had deserved the firing. But as between himself and Lane it had seemed the matter was forgotten.

Except, Frost told himself, it had not been forgotten, for there'd been the missing paper, the one that had slipped out of the envelope when he had opened it and which he had found, when he returned, on the floor beside his desk.

He remembered now, standing with the paper in his hand, knowing he should take it back to Lane. But if he took it back it would require another explanation and it would be embarrassing, and the paper did not seem to be of any great importance. Which was the case, he told himself, of half the stuff that went shuttling back and forth in the confidential files.

Some unremembered official, full of pomposity and with a penchant for cloak and dagger games, had started the system many years ago and it had been carried on and on, another of the moldy old traditions of the office routine. Some of it, of course, was of confidential nature, or at least semi-confidential, but the rest of it was simply inter-office matters with no need of secrecy attached.

So to avoid the embarrassment of another explanation, he had simply chucked the paper in a desk drawer and had forgotten it, knowing that if it had no more value than it seemed to have it would not be missed.

But he had made the wrong decision. Or it seemed so now.

And if what Appleton had done this morning was tied to the missing paper, then it was not only Appleton, but Lane involved as well.

He jerked open the center desk drawer and searched through the papers and the other junk and the paper was not there.

If he could only remember what was written on it! Something about putting something on some sort of list.

He wrinkled his brow, trying to remember. But the details still stayed fuzzy.

He searched the other drawers and there was no paper.

And that was how they'd known, he thought.

Someone had searched his desk and found it!

7

THE agent waved his arm at the tangle of underbrush and swamp.

"Twenty acres of it," he said. "And at the price we're asking, the best kind of investment that anyone can make. I tell you, friends, there is no better place you can put your money. In a hundred years it will bring ten times the price. In a thousand, if you could hang onto it that long, you'd be billionaires."

"But it's just a swamp," the woman said. "No one would ever want to build there and it can't be . . ."

"You're buying it today," the agent told her, "at so much an acre. Sell it a couple of hundred years from now and you'll be selling it at so much the foot. Just take the number of people there will be in the world by that time and compare their numbers to the total land area and you'll see what I mean. Once they get immortality and begin revivals . . ."

"But they won't need the land," the woman's husband said. "Once they get time travel, they'll send people back a million years to colonize the land, and when the land back there is filled, they'll send them back two million and . . ."

"Now, I tell you honestly," said the salesman, "I wouldn't count on that. There are a lot of people who have their doubts about time travel. Forever Center can get it, certainly, if it is possible, but if it's impossible, they won't get it. And if time travel is impossible, then this land will be worth a fortune. It doesn't matter that it's a little swampy. The human race will need every foot of land there is upon the earth. There'll come a time, perhaps, when the earth will be just one big building and . . ."

"But there's space travel, too," the woman said. "All those planets out there . . ."

"Madame," said the salesman, "let's be realistic for a moment. They've been out there for a hundred years or more and they have found no planets that a man could live on. Planets, of course, but nothing that anyone could live on without terraforming and terraforming takes a lot of time and money."

"Well, I don't know," the woman said. "This piece of swamp seems an awful gamble."

"Yes, it does," her husband said. "We just thought we'd look into it. We have been putting most of our money into stamps and we thought it might be a good idea to start spreading it around a little."

"Not that we have so awful much of it," the woman said. "Of money, I mean."

"Well, now, it's this way," said the salesman smoothly. "I'll agree that stamps may be a good investment. But how do you go about establishing title to them? Sure, you've got them and you put them away in a safety deposit vault or more when you are revived, for hobbies go in cycles. You go and get them and you probably can sell them at a likely profit. But a lot of people are buying stamps. The market might be glutted. Collecting stamps may not be done any more when you are revived for hobbies go in cycles. You might not get as much as you'd figured. You might, even, not be able to sell them at all. And if something had happened to them, how do you get them back? Say they were stolen, somehow. Even if you knew the one who'd took them and even if he still had them, how could you prove that they were yours? How could you recover them? There isn't any way to establish title to a stamp collection. And what if time had ruined them? What if they'd gotten damp or bacteria had got to work on them or any one of a dozen other things had happened? What have you got, then? I tell you, folks. You've got nothing. Absolutely nothing."

"That is right," the husband said. "I never thought of that. But the land would still be here and you'd have legal title."

"That's right," said the agent. "And to protect it through the years, all that you have to do is open an account with Forever Center and give us the right to draw on it to pay the taxes (which won't amount to much) or to cover costs necessary to protect the title.

"You see," he said, "it's very simple. We have it all worked out . . ."

"But," the woman said, "if it were only better land. If it weren't swamp."

"Now, I tell you," said the agent, "it doesn't make a bit of difference if it is swamp or not. In time to come, the world will need every foot of land. If not in a hundred years, then in a thousand. And if you want to, you can specify that you're to sleep a thousand years. Forever Center is glad to make that kind of stipulation. It will take them, probably, several hundred years, in any case, to just catch up when they start reviving people."

"You see," he said, "it's very simple. We have it all worked out . . ."

8

THE stamps had been from Switzerland and that meant the park bench in downtown Manhattan, and the time, penciled on the card, had been 1.30.

Joe Gibbons was already there and waiting when Frost came hurrying up the path.

"You're a little late," said Gibbons.

"I had to make sure," said Frost, "that I wasn't followed."

"Who would follow you? You've never worried before about being followed."

"Something came up at the office."

"Marcus sore at you? Afraid you might be undercutting him."

"That's ridiculous," said Frost.

"Yes, of course it is. But with a jerk like Marcus, you can't ever tell."

Frost sat down on the bench beside Gibbons.

A squirrel came questing down the path. Overhead a bird sang a single liquid note. The sky was polished blue and there was a quietness in the little park, a lazy sort of quietness.

"It's pleasant out here," said Frost. "A man should get out more often. Spend a half a day or so with nothing on his mind."

Gibbons said, "I've got something to tell you and I don't know quite how to go about it."

He had the air of a man with an unpleasant job and in a hurry to get it done. "The same thing has come up before," he said, "but I never mentioned it. I knew you wouldn't go for it. I knew you'd turn it down. . . ."

"Turn it down?"

"Dan," said Gibbons, gravely, "I have a proposition."

Frost shook his head. "Don't tell me."

37

Gibbons said, "I have to tell you this one. It's one you'll have to decide for yourself. It's too big. I can't decide it for you. I could turn the others down for you. I could say you didn't operate that way. But this one I can't. It's for a quarter million."

Frost said nothing. He made no move. It seemed suddenly that he had turned to stone and through the stoniness rang the shrilling stridence of alarm bells in his brain.

"I don't know," he finally said, but he only said the words as a cover-up, a chance to still the clapper banging in his skull, to get his thoughts together, to plan some sort of action.

"It's legitimate," said Gibbons. "I can handle it. Cold cash. No check. No record. Nothing. I can handle everything but the actual payoff. You are in on that."

"So I'll be tied to it," said Frost.

"So you're tied to it," said Gibbons. "Good God, man, they deserve that much for their quarter million. And besides, they wouldn't trust me with a quarter million. And you'd be crazy if you did. I could turn an awful heel for that kind of money. I couldn't help myself."

"And you? What kind of cut . . ."

Gibbons chuckled. "None. You keep the loot, every cent of it. Me, I get ten thousand for convincing you."

"We'd never get away with it," Frost said, sharply.

"I'm sorry, Dan. I had to tell you. I can go back and tell them no. Although, I'd hoped. I could lose ten thousand."

"Joe," said Frost, impulsively, "you've worked a long time with me. We have been friends . . ."

He stopped. He couldn't say what he had meant to say. It would do no good. For if Marcus Appleton had gotten to Joe Gibbons, there was nothing he could do about it.

"Yes, I know," said Gibbons. "We have been friends. I'd hoped you'd understand. And since you bring it up, we could get away with it. Me, it would be no problem for a guy like me. With you it might be a bit more difficult."

Frost nodded. "Invest the money, then apply for death."

"No! No!" protested Gibbons. "Not apply for death. They'd suspect something if you did. Arrange your death. A very natural death. Give me ten thousand of the loot and I'd get it done for you. That's the going rate. Very neat and easy. And the investment, of course, couldn't be in Forever stock. Something you could stash away—a bunch of paintings, maybe."

"You have to give me time," said Frost.

For he needed time. Time to get it figured out. Time to know what next to do.

"And if you didn't go for death," said Gibbons, "you could try to bluff it out. You've stopped a lot of them. This one just slipped past. You can't catch them all. No one expects you to."

"This one," said Frost, "must be a lulu. To rate a quarter million, it would have to be."

"I wouldn't kid you, Dan," said Gibbons. "This one would be dynamite. It would sell like wildfire. They figure a seven million mark in the first edition."

"You seem to know a lot about it."

"I made them talk to me," said Gibbons. "I wouldn't buy it blind. And they had to talk with me, for I was the only one who could channel it to you."

"It sounds to me you got in fairly deep."

"All right," said Gibbons. "I'll give it to you straight. I said a while ago I could go back and tell them no. But it wouldn't work that way. If you say no, I won't go back. Say no and walk away from here and I'll begin to travel. And I'll have to travel fast."

"You'd have to run for it," said Frost.

"I'd have to run for it."

They sat in silence. The squirrel sat up and watched them with its beady eyes, its forepaws hanging limply.

"Joe," said Frost, "tell me what it's all about."

"A book," Gibbons told him, "that claims Forever Center is a fraud, that the whole idea is a fraud. There's no chance of second life; there never was a chance. It was a thing dreamed up almost two hundred years ago to put an end to war . . ."

"Now, wait!" Frost exclaimed. "They can't . . ."

"They can," said Gibbons. "You could put a stop to it, of course, if you knew about it. Pressure could be brought and . . ."

"But I mean it can't be right!"

"What difference does it make?" asked Gibbons. "Right or wrong, it would be read. It would hit people where they live. It's no pamphlet job. This guy takes a scholarly approach. He's done a lot of research. He has good arguments. He has it documented. It may be a phony, but it doesn't look a phony. It's the kind of book a publisher would give his good right arm to publish."

"Or a quarter million."

"That's right. A quarter million."

"We can stop it now," said Frost, "but once it hits the stands, there wouldn't be a chance. Then we wouldn't dare. I can't let a book like that get by. I wouldn't dare to do it. I'd never live it down."

"You could work it," Gibbons reminded him, "so you wouldn't have to live it down."

"Even so," said Frost, "they could take retroactive action. They could pass the word along to overlook a certain man when time for revival came."

"They wouldn't do that," said Gibbons. "Memories don't run that long or bitter. But if you're afraid of that I could go in and clear your name. I could say I knew about the book but that you were knocked off before I could get it to you."

"For a price, of course."

"Dan," said Gibbons, sadly, "you said a while ago that we were friends. For a price, you say. That's no way for friends to talk. I'd do it out of friendship."

"One thing more," asked Frost. "Who is the publisher?"

"That's something I can't tell you."

"How can I . . ."

"Look, Dan, think it over. Don't say no right now. Give yourself twenty-four hours to think about it. Then come back and tell me."

Frost shook his head. "I don't need twenty-four hours. I need no time at all."

Gibbons stared at him glassily and for the first time, Frost could see, the man was shaken.

"Then I'll look you up. You may change your mind. For a quarter million! Man, it could set you up."

"I can't take the chance," said Frost. "Maybe you can, but I can't."

And he couldn't, he told himself.

For now the clanging clapper was no longer in his skull. Instead there was a coldness far worse than the clanging—the coldness of reason and of fear.

"Tell Marcus," he said, then hesitated. "No, don't tell Marcus. He'll find out for himself. He'll bust you, Joe, and don't you forget it. If he ever catches you . . ."

"Dan," yelled Gibbons, "what do you mean? What are you trying to say?"

"Nothing," said Frost. "Nothing at all. But if I were you, I'd start running now."

9

GLANCING through the half-open study door, Nicholas Knight saw the man enter the church, furtively, almost fearfully, with his hat clutched in both his hands and held foursquare across his chest.

Knight, seated at his desk, with the little study lamp pulled low against the desk top, watched in fascination.

The man, it was quite apparent, was unused to church and unsure of himself. He moved quietly and unsteadily down the aisle and he cast about him little probing glances, as if he might fear that some unknown and awesome shape would spring out at him from the pools of shadow.

And yet there was about him an attitude of worship, as if he might have come seeking refuge and comfort. And this, in itself, was something most unusual. For today few men came worshipfully. They came nonchalantly or with a calm assurance that said there was nothing here they needed, that they were only paying homage by an empty gesture to a thing that had become a cultural habit and very little more.

Watching the man, Knight felt something stir deep inside himself, a surge of feeling that he had forgotten could happen to a man—a sense of reaching out, a sense of benediction, of purpose and of duty and of pastoral compassion.

Of pastoral compassion, he thought. And where in a world like this was there any need of that? He had first sensed it long ago, when still in seminary, but he had not felt it since—for there had been no place for it and no need of it.

Silently, he rose from his chair and paced carefully and slowly to the door that led into the church.

The man had almost reached the front of the empty church and now he sidled from the aisle and sat down gingerly in a pew. His hat still was clutched against his breast and he sat forward, on the edge of the seat, his body stiff and straight. He stared straight ahead and the light of the candles flickering on the altar sent tiny shadows fleeing on his face.

For long minutes he sat there, unstirring. He scarcely seemed to breathe. And Knight, even from where he stood in the doorway of the study, imagined that he could feel the tension and the ache in that straight-held body.

And after those long moments of tensed sitting, the man rose to his feet and started back down the aisle again, hat still clutched tightly to his breast, marching out of the church exactly as he had entered it. There had not been, Knight was sure, at any time, a single flicker of expression in that frozen face, and the body was still as ramrod-straight, as uncompromising, as it had been before.

A man who had come inside seeking something and had not found it and now was leaving, knowing now, perhaps, that he would never find it.

Knight stepped out of the study and moved quietly toward the entrance. But the man, he saw, would reach the door, and be out, before he could intercept him.

He spoke softly: "My friend."

The man jerked around, fear etched upon his face.

"My friend," said Knight, "is there something I can do for you?"

The man mumbled, but he did not move. Knight moved closer to him.

"You need help," said Knight. "I am here to help you."

"I don't know," said the man. "I just saw the open door and came in."

"That door is never closed."

"I thought," said the man. "I hoped . . ."

His words ran out and he stood dumb and stupid.

"All of us must hope," said Knight. "All of us have faith."

"I guess that's it," said the man. "I haven't any faith. How does a man get faith? What is there for a man to have some faith in?"

"An everlasting life," Knight told him. "We must have faith in that. And in much else, besides."

The man laughed—a low, vicious, brutal laugh. "But we

43

have that already. We have everlasting life. And we do not need the faith."

"Not everlasting life," said Knight. "Just continued life. Beyond that continued life there is another life, a different kind of life, a better life."

The man raised his head and his eyes grew hard, like two small points of fire.

"You believe that, Shepherd? You are the shepherd, aren't you?"

"Yes, I am the shepherd. And yes, I do believe it."

"Then what sense does all this make—this continuation? Wouldn't it be better . . ."

Knight shook his head. "I don't know," he said. "I can't pretend to know. But I can't bring myself to question God's purpose in allowing it."

"But if He allows it, why?"

"Perhaps a longer life to prepare ourselves the better when our time does come to die."

"They talk," said the man, "of life forever, of immortality, of no need of dying. Then what's the use of God? We won't need the other life, for we'll already have it."

"Yes," said Knight, "perhaps we will. But then we'll cheat ourselves. And the immortality that they talk about may not be something that we want. We may grow tired of it."

"And you, Shepherd? What of you?"

"What of me? I don't understand."

"Which of these other lives for you? Are you freezer-bound?"

"Why, I . . ."

"I see," the other said. "Good day, Shepherd, and many thanks for trying."

CLIFFORD D. SIMAK

have that already. We have everlasting life. And we do not
need the faith."

10

FROST wearily climbed the stairs and let himself into his
room. He closed the door behind him and hung up his hat.
He slumped into an old and battered easy chair and stared
about the room.

And for the first time in his life, the poverty and the
squalor of it struck him across the face.

The bed stood in one corner and in another corner a tiny
stove and a keeper for his stock of food. A mangy carpet,
with holes worn here and there, made an ignoble effort to
cover the bareness of the floor. A small table stood before
the one lone window and here he ate and wrote. There were
several other chairs and a narrow chest of drawers and the
open door of a tiny closet, where he stored his clothes. And
that was all there was.

This is the way we live, he thought. Not myself alone, but
many billion others. Not because we want to, not because
we like it. But because it is a wretched way of life we've
imposed upon ourselves, a meanness and a poverty, a down
payment on a second life—the fee, perhaps, for immortality.

He sat, sunk in bitterness, half drowsy with his bitterness
and hurt.

A quarter million dollars, he thought, and he'd had to
turn it down. Not, he admitted to himself, that he was
above the taking of it, not because of any nobleness, but
because of fear. Fear that the entire setup had been no
more than a trap devised by Marcus Appleton.

Joe Gibbons, he told himself, was a friend and a faithful
worker, but Joe's friendship could be bought if the sum
were great enough. All of us, he thought with the sour
taste of truth lying in his mouth, can be bought. There was
no man in the world who was not up for sale.

And it was, he told himself, because of the price that

45

each must pay for that second life, the grubbing and the saving and the misery that was banked as a stake to start the second life.

It all had started less than two centuries before—in 1964, by a man named Ettinger. Why, asked Ettinger, did man need to die? Die now of cancer, when a cure for cancer might be only ten years off? Die now of old age when old age was no more than an ailment that in another hundred years might be susceptible to cure?

It was ridiculous, said Ettinger. It was a pity and a waste and fraud. There was no need of death. There was a way to beat it.

Men had talked of it before, had speculated on it, but it had been Ettinger who had said: Let us do something—now!

Let's develop a technique by which those who die can be frozen and stored away against that day when the maladies of which they died can be treated medically. Then, when this is possible, revive the dead, wipe away the ravages of old age, banish the malignancy of cancer, repair the weakened heart, and give them all a second chance at life.

The idea had been slow to gain acceptance, had been ignored by all except a few, had gathered guffaws on television shows, had been treated gingerly by writers who did not want to identify themselves with the fringe of fanaticism.

Slow to gain acceptance, but it grew. It grew stubbornly as the dedicated few labored day and night to do the necessary basic research, to devise the technology that was necessary, to erect the installations, and to perfect the organization that would hold it all together.

The years went on and the idea crept into the consciousness of men—that death might be defeated, that death was not an end, that not only a spiritual but a physical second life was possible. That it was there for those who wanted it, that it was no longer just a long-range gamble, but a business proposition with a good chance of success.

Still no one would say publicly that they were about to take advantage of it, for in the public image it was still a crackpot scheme. But as the years went on more and more made surreptitious contracts and when they died were frozen and were stacked away against the day of their revival.

And each of those who was stacked away left in trust with the organization built so painfully from nothing, the pittance or the fortune they had scraped together in their lifetime, to be invested until that time when they would be revived.

There had been a congressional inquiry in Washington, which had come to nothing, and a question had been raised on the floor of Commons, which likewise came to nothing. The movement still was regarded crackpot, but it had the virtue of being non-obnoxious. It did not push itself, it did not foist itself upon the public consciousness, it did no preaching. And while more and more it became a matter of private conversation and of public interest, it was paid no official heed, possibly because officialdom did not know just what attitude to take. Or perhaps because, like the ancient UFO squabble, it was too controversial to touch.

Just when it happened, or how it happened, or what brought about the realization, no one now could tell—but there came the day when it became apparent that the little movement of 1964, now called Forever Center, had become the biggest thing the world had ever known.

Big in many ways. Big in the hold it had on the public imagination, which, in many instances, now constituted a firm belief in not only the purpose of the program but in its capacity to carry out the program. Big in the participation in the program, with millions of frozen bodies stored away to await revival. And, perhaps most important of all, big in its assets and investments.

For all those millions who now lay frozen had left their funds in trust with Forever Center. And one day the world woke to find that Forever Center was the largest stockholder of the world and that in many instances it had gained control of vast industrial complexes.

Now, too late, the governments (all the governments) realized they were powerless to do anything about Forever Center, if, in fact, they had wanted to do anything about it. For to investigate it, to license, to restrict it in any way would have been flying not only into the face of an entrenched financial position but also into the face of an awakened public interest.

47

So there was nothing done and Forever Center became more powerful and more invulnerable. And today, thought Frost, it was the government of the world and the financial institution of the world and the world's only hope.

But a hope that was dearly paid for—a hope that had made tightfisted moneygrubbers of the people of the world.

He'd gone without a pint of milk—a pint of milk he'd wanted, a pint of milk that his body had cried out for—when he ate his lunch. And that lunch had been two thin sandwiches from a paper bag. And all of this because each week he must put away a good part of his salary in Forever stock, so that during those long years when he lay dead and frozen the funds would multiply by interest and by dividend. He lived in this wretched room and he ate cheap food, he had never married.

But his fund against revival and the second life grew week by week and his whole life centered on the credit book that showed his ownership of stock.

And this afternoon, he recalled, he had stood ready to sell Forever Center and his position with Forever Center for a quarter million dollars—more money than he could hope to accumulate in his entire lifetime. He had been ready, even willing, to take the money, then, if necessary, to deliberately seek death.

The only thing that had stopped him was the fear that it was a trap.

And had it been a trap? he wondered.

If it had been a trap, why had the trap been set? For what reason had Marcus Appleton become his enemy?

The missing paper? And if that were the case, what made the paper so important—so important that he must be discredited before he tried to use it.

For if the paper were important and somehow incriminating, they'd expect that in his own good time he'd put it to his use. For that is what they would have done themselves. That was what anyone would do—anything at all to squeeze out that extra dollar, to gain a preferred position that would mean an extra dollar.

He'd chucked the paper in the desk and now, today, when he'd hunted for it, it had not been there. And if they'd gotten the paper back, then why . . .

But wait a minute. Had he chucked the paper in the desk? Or had he stuffed it in his pocket?

He crouched deeper in the chair and tried hard to remember. But he could not remember with any clarity. He might have put it in his pocket instead of in the desk. Or he might have tossed it in the wastebasket. He could not be sure.

If he'd put it in his pocket, it might still be here. It still might be in the pocket of his other suit, although that seemed most unlikely, for he'd sponged and pressed the suit just a week or so ago, and hung it carefully away. When he'd done that, he would have cleaned out the pockets and put the stuff he found in them in one of the dresser drawers for a later sorting out.

If that were the case, he still might have the paper. It might be in a dresser drawer.

And if he had that paper it still might be possible to use it. It could, conceivably, be a club against Appleton and Lane.

He heaved himself out of the chair and crossed to the chest of drawers. He jerked out the top drawer and there lay a cluttered fistful of paper that he had taken from the suit.

He picked up the papers and started shuffling through them, breath rasping in his throat in his eagerness.

A sharp rap sounded on the door and he swung about defensively and fear hit him in the stomach. For no one ever came rapping at his door. No one ever came to visit.

He jammed the sheaf of papers into the inside pocket of his jacket and closed the drawer.

The rapping came again, louder and insistent.

11

Good day, Shepherd, the man had said. Good day, Shepherd, and many thanks for trying.

This frightened, unsure man who had come seeking comfort and assurance and who had left with neither comfort nor assurance. This man had turned to him, thought Nicholas Knight, the first time a man had turned to him for help in many, many years. And he had failed the man, for there'd been no help to give.

It would have been so easy to give the help, Knight told himself. So easy to give the comfort and assurance. For another shepherd, perhaps, but not for Nicholas Knight. For Nicholas Knight, himself, lacked the comfort and assurance.

He sat hunched over his desk, with the study lamp bent low to make a tiny pool of light upon the polished desk top. He had sat hunched there for what had seemed to be hours. And in that endless time the one raw thought ran like a red-hot saw across his brain: He had failed the one man who had ever come to him for help.

He had failed him because there was in himself the same blank emptiness there was in all the world. He professed a faith and he had no faith. He paid lip service to spiritual immortality, but he had never found it in himself to foreswear the physical immortality that was held out as a promise by Forever Center.

The church stood—not this one structure, but all the similar structures in the world, all the vast ecclesiastical organization—for something that was above and beyond the mere physical gropings of blind men. It and the forerunners of it had so stood, no matter how mistaken, since time immemorial. From crude beginnings, from the witch doctor in the jungle, from the human sacrifices in the sacred groves, the church had always stood for something that the grasp of man could never reach. It had stood for the mystery of mind, for the ecstasy of spirit, for the hard, clear intellectual light.

But it stood so no longer, Nicholas Knight said to himself. The church never had been more than the men who made it. Today there were no dedicated men, no steadfast potential martyrs, strong in faith and willing to die, if need be, for the upholding of their faith. Today the church was compromise and expediency, manned by men of little faith.

If a man could only pray, he thought. But there was no point in praying when the prayer was never more than a mouthful of ritualistic words. Man prayed with his heart, he thought, never with his tongue.

He stirred uneasily and dropped his hand into the pocket of his cassock. His fingers closed upon the rosary and he pulled it out and laid it on the table.

The wooden beads were worn and polished from much handling and the metal crucifix was dull and tarnished.

Men still prayed by such as this, he knew, but not as many as had at one time. For the old established church at Rome, perhaps the one and only church that still retained some remnant of its old significance, had fallen on bad days. Most men today, if they paid any service to formalized religion, paid it to the new church that had risen—the formalized and impersonal reminder (and remainder) of what once had been religion.

Here was faith, he thought, fingering the rosary. Here was blind and not-quite-understanding faith, but a better thing than no faith at all.

The rosary had come down to him, down through the family, generation after generation, and there was, he recalled, an old story that went with it—how an old grandmother, many times removed, in some forgotten village in Central Europe, had been bound for church when a sudden rain came up, and how she had sought shelter in a nearby cottage, and after gaining shelter had, on impulse, thrust the rosary out the door, commanding the rain to stop. And the rain had stopped and the sun came out. And how all the days she lived she had held perfect faith that the rosary stopped the rain. And how others, long after she had died, had told of the incident, also in perfect faith.

This, of course, Knight told himself, was no more than the mere trappings of faith, but it, at least, was something.

If he had held only a portion of the faith of that old grandmother, he could have helped the man. The one man, in all the thousands he had known, who had ever felt the need of faith.

Why should this one man, one in many thousands, so stand in need of faith? What mental mechanism, what driving spiritual sense had impelled him on his hunt for faith?

He conjured up the face of the man again—the horror-haunted eyes, the unruly shock of hair, the sharp, high cheekbones.

It was a face he knew. The face, perhaps, of empty man —a lumping together of all the faces he had ever seen.

But it was not that entirely. It was not the universal face. It was an individual face, a face that he had seen, and not too long ago.

Suddenly it came clear—the memory sharp and hard— this same face staring out at him from the front page of the morning paper.

And this, he thought, in sudden terror at his own inadequacy, was the man that he had failed—a man who had nothing left but faith, absolutely nothing in the world but the hope of faith.

The man who had come into the church and had left again, as empty when he left as when he entered, perhaps emptier, for then even hope was gone, had been Franklin Chapman.

12

Frost jerked the door open in a sudden, violent motion, his body tensed and ready for whoever might be standing there and knocking.

A woman stood there, cool and poised, the faint light of the hall bulb glinting in the blackness of her hair.

"Are you Mr. Frost?" she asked.

Frost gulped in astonishment, perhaps even in relief.

"Yes, I am," he said. "Will you please step in?"

She stepped through the doorway.

"I do hope," she said, "that I'm not intruding. My name is Ann Harrison and I'm an attorney."

"Ann Harrison," he said, "I am pleased to meet you. Aren't you the one . . ."

"Yes, I am," she said. "I defended Franklin Chapman."

"I saw the pictures in the paper. I should have recognized you at once."

"Mr. Frost," she said, "I'll be honest with you. I sneaked up on you. I could have phoned, but you might have refused to see me, so I took the chance of coming here. I hoped you wouldn't throw me out."

"I wouldn't throw you out," said Frost. "There is no reason that I should. Won't you take a chair?"

She sat down in the chair he had been sitting in. She was beautiful, he thought, but there was a strength behind the beauty, and there was a hardness in her, in a polished sort of way.

"I need your help," she said.

He went to another chair, sat down, took his time to answer.

"I don't quite follow you," he said.

"I got a tip-off you were a decent sort of man, that one could talk to you. You were the man to see, they told me."

53

"They?"

She shook her head. "It doesn't matter. Just talk around the town. Will you listen to me?"

"Yes," he said, "I'll listen. As for being any help . . ."

"We'll see," she said. "It's about Franklin Chapman . . ."

"You did all you could for him," said Frost. "He didn't have too much going for him."

"That's the point," she said. "Someone else might have done better, I don't know. The point is that it wasn't justice."

"It was law," said Frost.

"Yes, it was that. And I live by the law. Or I should live by it. But the legal profession is in a good position to distinguish between law and justice and the two are not the same. There can be no justice in denying a man a second chance at life. Certainly, due to circumstances beyond his control, Chapman arrived too late at a scene of death and, as a result, a woman lost her second chance at life. But to decree that Chapman also should be denied that second life is wrong. It's the old jungle law, again. An eye for an eye, a tooth for a tooth. As an intelligent race, we should be beyond all that. Is there no such a thing as mercy? Is there no compassion? Do we have to go back to tribal law?"

"We're in an interregnum," said Frost. "We're shifting from our old way of life to a new condition of life. The old rules don't apply and it's too soon to apply any new ones. We had to set up rules which would carry us over the transition period. And those rules had to assure one thing beyond all question, that the new generations take care of the old to the extent that nothing interfered with the revival plan. There had to be some sort of assurance that everyone who died would be guaranteed his chance at revival. If we fail one person, then we've violated a trust and the pledge we've made to everyone. The only way to provide that kind of assurance was to formulate a code of law which provided a penalty harsh enough to make certain the pledge being carried out."

"It might have been better," said Ann Harrison, "if Chapman had applied for trial by drug. I suggested it, I even urged it. But he refused. There are certain kinds of people who rebel against laying themselves, their whole life, all their motives and their drives, open to legal scrutiny. In certain types of crime—treason, for example—trial by drug is mandatory, but in this case it was not. I have a feeling it would have been better if it had been."

"I still fail to see the point of this," said Frost. "I don't see how I can help you."

"If I could convince you," she said, "that some sort of mercy were permissible, then you'd be in a position to take it up with Forever Center. If Forever Center indicated to the court . . .

"Now, just a moment," said Frost. "I'm in no position to do a thing like that. I head promotion and publicity and have no concern with policy."

"Mr. Frost," she said, "I have been quite frank about why I came to you. I understood you were the one man at Center who would give me time, who would listen to me. So I came to you and I don't mind being honest with you. I have a selfish purpose. I am fighting for my client. I'll do anything that's possible to help him."

"Does he know you're here?"

She shook her head. "He wouldn't like it if he knew. He's a strange man, Mr. Frost. He has a deep and stubborn pride. He would never beg. But I'll beg if I have to."

"Would you do this for every client?" asked Frost. "I don't think you would. What's so special about this one?"

"It's not the way you may be thinking," she said. "Although I won't resent your thinking it. But the man has something that you so seldom find. An inner dignity, the strength to meet adversity without asking quarter. He fairly breaks your heart. And he was trapped—trapped by a set of laws that we legislated a hundred years or more ago in an excessive burst of enthusiasm and determination that nothing must upset the great millennium. In principle, good laws, perhaps, but they're outmoded now. They worked as a deterrent; they have served their purpose. I've checked and since this particular law was passed less than twenty people have been given death. So it must have served its purpose. It has helped to mold the kind of society that we wanted—or that we thought we wanted. There is no reason now for the penalty to be enforced to its full extent.

"And there's another reason I feel so strongly. I went with him when they removed the transmitter from his chest. Have you ever . . ."

"But that," protested Frost, "was far beyond the call of your obligation. There was no reason that you should."

"Mr. Frost," she said, "when I accept a case I commit myself. I stand by my client all the way. I never quite quit caring."

"Like now," he said.

"Like now. I stood there with him and watched the sentence carried out. Physically, of course, it's nothing. Just beneath the skin. Just above the heart. It records the heartbeat and sends out a signal and that signal is recorded on a monitor and when the signal stops a rescue squad is sent. And they took it out and tossed it on a little metal tray that held the instruments and there it was, a little metallic thing, but it wasn't just a piece of metal; it was a man's life laying there. Now there's no indication of his heartbeat on the monitor and when he dies there'll be no rescue squad. They talk about another thousand years of life, another million years of life, they talk about forever. But there's no million years, no forever for my client. He has only forty years, maybe less than that."

"And what would you do?" asked Frost. "Simply implant the transmitter once again . . ."

"No, of course not. The man committed a crime and must pay for it. This is simple justice, but it need not be vicious justice. Why can't the sentence be commuted to ostracism? That is bad enough, but it's not execution, it's not death."

"Almost as bad as death," said Frost. "Branded on both cheeks and read out of the human race. No one can communicate with you, no one can traffic with you—even for the necessities of life. You are shorn of all possessions, left only with the clothes you stand in."

"But not death," said Ann Harrison. "You still have the transmitter in your chest. The rescue squad will come."

"And you expect that I can do this, that I can swing a commutation?"

She shook her head. "Not just like that," she said. "Not overnight, not tomorrow or the next day. But I need a friend at Center, Chapman needs a friend at Center. You'd know who to talk with and when to talk with them, you'd know what was going on, you'd know when something could be done—that is, if I can convince you, if I can make you see it as I see it. And don't mistake me. You won't be paid for it. There are no funds to pay you. If you do it, you'll have to do it because you think it's right."

"I suspected that," said Frost. "I would imagine you've not been paid, yourself."

"Not a cent," she said. "He wanted to, of course. But he has a family and he's not been able to put away too much. He showed me his holdings and they are pitiful. I couldn't send his wife into the second life a pauper. For himself, of course, there's now no need of savings. He's still got his job, but in the face of public opinion, he won't hold it long. And where does he go to get another job?"

"I don't know," said Frost. "I could talk with . . ."

And then he stopped. For who could he talk with? Not Marcus Appleton. Not after what had happened. Not Peter Lane, if Appleton and Lane were, indeed, involved in the matter of the missing paper, a paper which, incidentally, might be no longer missing. B.J.? It didn't seem too likely that B.J. would listen—or any of the rest of them.

"Miss Harrison," he told her, "you probably came to the one man in Forever Center the least likely to be of help to you."

"I'm sorry," she said. "I didn't mean to put you on the spot. If you can be of any help, even if you're no more than willing to try to help, I will appreciate it. For even an expression of a willingness to help will do something to restore my confidence, will let me know that someone still remains who has a sense of fairness."

"If I can be of any help," said Frost, "I'm inclined to do it. But I won't stick out my neck, you understand. Right at the moment, I can afford no trouble."

"That," said Ann, "is good enough for me."

"I'm promising nothing."

"I can't expect you to. You'll do what you can."

It was wrong, thought Frost. He had no right to offer help. He had no business mixing into this at all. And especially he had no right to offer help when he knew there was nothing he could do.

But the dingy room somehow seemed the warmer now, and brighter. It was a sense of life and living such as he had not known before. And he knew it was this woman sitting in the room who gave it warmth and light, but a dying warmth and light, like a warmth and light given off by a dying fire. In time, when she had left, once the memory had worn thin, the room again would become cold and dingy, as it had been before.

"Miss Harrison," he asked, suddenly, "could I take you out to dinner?"

She smiled and shook her head.

"I'm sorry," Frost said. "I had hoped, perhaps . . ."

"Not out," she said. "I can't have you spending that much money on me. But if you have food here, I can cook."

13

NESTOR BELTON closed the book and shoved it across the desk, away from him. He lowered his head and put up his fists to knuckle at tired eyeballs.

Examinations tomorrow, he thought, and he should get some sleep. But there was so much that he needed to review, if no more than a quick and skimpy check through the pages of the texts.

For these examinations were important. From those scoring highest would be chosen those students who would be allowed to enter the School of Counseling. Ever since he could remember he had wanted to be a counselor. And it was more important now than it had ever been, for there was heard from every quarter rumors that in the matter of just a few more years immortality would become a fact, that the men at Forever Center had finally cracked the problem and all that now remained was a perfection of the necessary techniques.

Once immortality became possible, revivals would begin and then the corps of counselors would be put to work. For years they had been held in reserve against the need of them and there had been many of them who had lived out lifetimes of waiting, without a thing to do, and now, themselves, were stored in vaults, waiting for revival.

The counselors and the revival technicians, two groups of men, thousands of them, who had stood by and waited all these years, always ready for the day when the waiting hordes of dead could be brought back to life again. Two corps of men who had been trained at the expense of Forever Center and who had stood by, being paid for doing nothing because there was nothing yet to do.

But ready, always ready. One with the acre after acre of empty tiers of housing, built against the day when there would be need of them. One with the great storehouses filled with food, turned out by the converters, stored and waiting against Revival Day.

For, Nestor Belton told himself, Forever Center thought of everything, had planned only as a devoted institution manned by devoted and unselfish men could plan. For almost two hundred years the Center had been custodian of the dead, guardian of mankind's hope, architect of the life to come.

He rose from his desk and walked to the single window in his student's cubicle. Outside a pale moon, half obscured by floating clouds, made a misty landscape of the dormitory yard. And far off, toward the west and north, rose the massive shaft of Forever Center.

He was glad, he told himself for the thousandth time, that he had been so lucky as to have a view of the Center from his window. For it was an inspiration and a promise and a seeming benediction. He had only to look out the window to know what he was working for, to glimpse a reminder of the glory that after almost a million years (although there were some who said more than a million years) would crown the long, slow crawl of man from the mindless primal ooze.

Eternal life, Nestor Belton told himself; no need ever to die, but to keep on and on and in a body that would be always youthful. To have the time to develop one's intellect and knowledge to the full capacity of the human brain. To gather wisdom, but not age. To have the time to carry out all the work that the mind could dream. To compose great music, write great books, to paint finally the kind of canvases that artists had always tried to paint, but usually had failed, to go out to the stars, to explore the galaxy, to dig to the root of meaning in the atom and the cosmos, to watch lofty mountains wear away and others rise, to see rivers dwindle down to nothing and other rivers form, and when, ten billion years from now, flaming death reached out for this solar system, to have been gone to other systems far in the depth of space.

Nestor Belton hugged himself, thin arms wrapped around thin chest.

This was the time to be alive, he thought.

And he thought in horror of those days when men had

died and stayed dead, when there had been no thought of other life beyond the frail and tottering promise of a medieval faith that tried to make of faith the very stuff of knowing.

All those other poor dead people, who had died without assurance that death was only temporary—who had feared death as an end and nothingness, who had feared it in spite of their oft protested faith, who had shrunk from it and thrust it back into an obscure place within their minds each time they thought of it, because they did not want to think of it, could not bear to think of it.

A thin wind fretted at the eaves above him and it was a lonely sound. The shadows of the yard were diluted shadows that seemed to have no substance. The far-off whiteness of Forever Center was a misty light against the night-black sky. As if, he thought, dawn might not be too far distant. And that was how it must have seemed at times, he told himself, to the men of Forever Center working toward the dawn. But encountering setbacks and disappointments when it seemed that the final accomplishments were within their grasp. Now, however, from what one heard, from the filtered rumor spoken everywhere, dawn (no false dawn this time) was at last in sight and man in a few more years would have been brought to that final perfection of purpose and expression that had been inherent in that first feeble thread of life born in the primal seas.

And he, Nestor Belton, hopefully would have a hand in it. He and the other counselors, when the people were revived, would perform the necessary function of rehabilitation, so that the revived could fit into the present culture.

But to do a job like that, a man must know so much, must be so thoroughly trained as an accomplished historian, with an especial knowledge of the last two centuries.

Six long years of study—if he ranked high enough in the exams that he faced tomorrow.

He took one last look at the misty whiteness of Forever Center and went back to his books.

14

THE dinner tapers flickered, almost burned out, and the scent of roses filled the dingy room—although, in the candlelight, the room was not so dingy. And both of them, the tapers and the roses, had spelled extravagance, but Frost found that he could not regret the money they had cost. It was the first time in years that he had not eaten alone and he could not remember any evening as pleasant as this one had turned out to be.

Ann Harrison had not again referred to the Chapman matter, but there had been much to talk about—the European art exhibit at the Metropolitan Museum of Art (they both, it turned out, had been to see it, on one of the free days); the new historical novel that everyone was talking about, a romance of the early days of space flight; the unreasonable attitude of the traffic cops; the wisdom of investing in other commodities than Forever stock—and themselves.

Ann had been born and reared in Manhattan, she told him, had completed her law course at Columbia, had spent one vacation in France and another in Japan, but now no longer took vacations, for it was a waste of time and money, and aside from this, her law practice now took all her time—too much work for one person, not enough for two.

And he, in turn, had told her about the vacations he had spent as a boy, on his grandfather's farm in Wisconsin, no longer a farm, of course, for there were no farms, but a sort of family summer place.

"Although," he said, "it isn't even a summer place now. The family doesn't own it. At the time of my grandparents' death it was sold to one of the big land companies and the proceeds turned into Forever stock. I went out to Chicago several years ago on business and took a day off and drove up to the place. It's way out west, on the bluffs above a little town named Bridgeport. The buildings still were standing, but there was no one there, of course, and the place is beginning to look shabby and rundown."

"It seems a shame," said Ann, "that there aren't any farms. All that land going back to wilderness. You'd think that the government would encourage farming. It would supply a lot of people with employment."

He shook his head. "I regret it, too. There was something solid about a farm. And a nation without farms seems a sort of shaky setup. But there really was no reason to keep them going and there is all sort of reason to tool up the converter plants to full capacity. We'll need those plants, and in operating order, when revivals start. So far as employment is concerned . . ."

"Yes, I know," she said. "All the facilities to be built. Block after block of apartments and each one standing empty. Not only here, but in all the world. When I was in Japan they were building acres of them."

"We'll need them all," he told her. "Almost a hundred billion frozen and a present population not much less than half of that."

"Where are we going to put them all?" she asked. "I know that . . ."

"Bigger buildings, if necessary. Forever Center is a bit better than a mile in height. It was built as a model, really, to see if a building that large could be built and stand. And it seems to be all right. There was a little settling to start with, but nothing too alarming. You can't build that high everywhere, of course. It depends on the basement rock. But the engineers now are saying that if you go deep enough . . ."

"You mean living underground?"

"Well, yes, both under and above. Go deep enough to find good underpinning, then build up from there, as high as you can build. That way, you can take care of, say, several million people in a single building. What would be the equivalent of a small city in a single structure."

"But there is a limit."

"Oh, certainly," he agreed. "There will come a time,

some centuries from now, even with the best that we can do, when there'll no longer be any room."

"And then we migrate into time?"

"Well, yes," he said, "we hope so."

"You haven't got it yet?"

"Not yet," he said, "but close."

"And immortality?"

"Ten years," he said. "Twenty maybe. Unless we hit a snag."

"Dan," she said, "was it smart, the way we did it—to keep all those people frozen until we could hand them immortality? We know what to do with cancer, how to repair the weakened heart, how to handle old age. We could have started revivals almost a hundred years ago, but we just keep on, stacking up the bodies. We said what difference does it make if they sleep a little longer. They will never know. So let us make it worth their while, let's give them a surprise, those old ones, when they wake up. Let's give them life eternal."

He laughed. "I don't know. You can't get me to argue that one. Too many words already have been wasted on it. Personally, I don't see what difference it could make."

"But with all those billions, think of all the time that it will take. Each one of them must be processed . . ."

"I know, but there are corps of technicians, thousands of them, ready to start work the moment that the word is given. And there are other corps of counselors standing by."

"But it will take time."

"Yes," he said. "It will take a lot of time. It would have been simpler, the way it first was planned. But then along came this social security business. I know it was the only fair way, for you couldn't put a price on extended life. But it makes the chore of revival so much harder and I hate to think of the economic chaos."

"It'll be worked out," she said. "It has to be. As you say, it is only fair. You can't have immortality only for those who can afford to pay for it."

"But think of India," he said. "Think of Africa and China. People who even now can't earn a decent living, kept from starving by world relief programs. Not a dime to lay away. Not a cent invested. They'll be revived into a world that, for them, will be no better than this life they know right now. They still will face starvation; they still will stand in line for food handouts. All the social security program gives them is their shot at immortality. It gives them nothing more."

"It's better than death," she said. "It's better than an end to everything."

"I suppose it is," he said.

She glanced at her watch. "I'm sorry," she said, "but it is time to go. It's way past time, in fact. I don't know when I've enjoyed an evening quite so much."

"I wish you'd stay a little longer."

She shook her head and rose from the table. "I never intended to stay at all. But I am glad I did. I'm glad it worked out the way it did."

"Some other time, perhaps," he suggested. "I could phone you."

"That would be nice of you."

"I'll see you home."

"I have my car downstairs."

"Ann, there's one thing more."

Half turned toward the door, she hesitated.

"I've been thinking," he said. "You're an attorney. I may have need of one. Would you represent me?"

She turned to face him, half puzzled, half laughing. "What earthly need would you have of an attorney?"

"I don't know," he said. "I may not really need one. But I think I have a certain paper. I have a bunch of papers. I'm almost certain it's among them. But I have a feeling it might be better if I didn't look, if I didn't know . . ."

"Dan," she asked, "what in the world are you trying to say?"

"I'm not quite sure. You see, I have this paper, or I think I have it."

"Well, what's so great about it? What kind of paper is it?"

"I don't know what kind of paper. Just a note, a memo. But I shouldn't have it. It doesn't belong to me."

"Get rid of it," she told him. "Burn it. There's no need . . ."

65

"No!" he protested. "No, I can't do that. It might be important."

"Certainly you must know what is written on it. You must know . . ."

He shook his head. "I looked at it when it first fell into my hands, but I didn't understand it then. And now I've forgotten what was written on it. At first it didn't seem important . . ."

"But now it does," she said.

He nodded. "Maybe. I don't know."

"And you don't want to know."

"I guess that's it," he said.

She crinkled up her face at him, half humorously, half seriously. "I can't see how I fit into this."

"I thought that if I took all the papers, the bundle that I spoke of, and put them in an envelope and gave the envelope to you . . ."

"As your attorney?"

He nodded miserably

She hesitated. "Would I know more about that particular piece of paper? Would you tell me more?"

"I don't think I should," he said. "I wouldn't want to implicate you. I have the papers in my pocket. I was looking for this certain paper—to be sure I had it. I found a bunch of papers I'd taken out of my other suit when you arrived. So I stuffed the papers in my pocket . . ."

"You were afraid someone was coming to take the paper from you."

"Yes. Something like that. I don't know what I thought. But now I realize that perhaps it would be better if I didn't know what was in the paper or even where it was."

"I'm not too sure," she said, "of either the ethics or legality."

"I understand," he said. "It was a bad idea. Let's forget about it."

"Dan," she said.

"Yes."

"I asked you a favor."

"And I couldn't do it."

"You will when you can."

"Don't count on me. The chances are . . ."

"You're in trouble, Dan."

"Not yet. I suppose I could be. You used poor judgment. You came to the one man the least likely to be of help to you."

"I don't think so," she said. "I'll gamble on you. Now, let's get that envelope . . ."

15

Amos Hicklin picked up another short length of wood and placed it on the fire. The fire was a woodsman's fire, small and neat.

Supper was finished and the frying pan and coffeepot had been washed at the edge of the moon-burnished river, with a handful of sand serving for the soap. And now was the time, with the darkness settling in, for a man to prop himself against a tree trunk and smoke a pipe as it should be smoked, slowly and leisurely, giving space for thought.

From up a wooded hollow a lone whippoorwill took up its evening song, a plaintive questioning call that had something otherworldly in it. Out in the river a fish splashed loudly as it leaped out of the water to snare an insect that had skimmed the water's surface.

Hicklin reached out to his tidy woodpile and picked up two more sticks and placed them carefully on the fire. Then he settled back against his tree trunk and took from his shirt pocket his pipe and tobacco pouch.

This was good, he thought—June and pleasant weather, moon shining on the river, an old whippoorwill chunking up the hollow, and the mosquitoes not too bad.

And tomorrow, maybe . . .

It was a crazy place, he thought, for a man to hide a treasure, on an island in a river. A risky place to hide anything of value, for any fool should know what could happen to an island.

Yet it made a zany sort of sense. The man had been on the lam and was very nearly trapped and he had to hide the stuff any way, or any place, he could. And it had the added advantage of being one of the last places in the world where anyone ever would suspect a treasure had been hidden. For the islands here were little more than sandbars which in the course of time had been overgrown by shallow-rooted willows. They might exist for years or they might vanish in a night, for this was a treacherous river, with shifting currents and changing undertows.

It well might be a wild goose chase, Hicklin knew, but the stakes were large and he was losing nothing but a year or so of time. A year of time against, roughly estimated, a cool one million dollars.

Jade, he thought. What a crazy thing to steal!

For in the day that it had been stolen there'd have been little chance of getting rid of it—unique museum pieces which would be recognized almost anywhere as stolen offerings.

Yet, perhaps, Steven Furness had never meant to sell it. There was such a thing, perhaps, as falling so in love with beauty that he'd want it for his own. Working for years in the museum, he may have resented, in his twisted mind, pieces of such loveliness suffering exposure to the vulgar public gaze.

He had almost made it. If he had not been recognized in that backwoods crossroad eating place by some farm kid who had seen his picture in a paper, on that day almost two hundred years ago, he would have got away with it. And in a sense, he had got away with it, for he'd not been captured, but had lived out his life, an old, white-haired, doddering man who had scraped out a precarious existence by performing jobs, all highly questionable, in the dives of New Orleans.

Hicklin sat in the night, his legs stretched straight out in front of him, puffing slowly at his pipe, the flicker of the campfire making light and shadow on his face.

A howling wilderness, he thought. All this land, farmed for so long, gone back to wilderness. For there was now no use of land except for living space and the population which had at one time made a living off the land now was congregated where the jobs were, in the great metropolitan centers, squeezed together in the little rooms and flats, living in another wilderness of the human animal. The entire Eastern seaboard, one vast sea of humans, living cheek by jowl; Chicago, the vast Midwest megalopolis clustered around Lake Michigan as far north as old Green Bay and swinging deep around the eastern shore; and the several other centers of massive populations, great islands of jammed humanity growing ever bigger.

And here he was, he thought—a man apart from this, one of the few men who were apart from it. But driven by the same motives and same greed as all those other billions. Although there was one difference. He was a gambler and they were drudging slaves.

A gamble, he thought. It could be a gamble. But the letter written on the deathbed and the rude, scrawled map, despite their romantic character, had a strange, sure ring of authenticity. And his search of the records had borne out the facts of the last days of Steven Furness. There was no doubt at all that he had been the man who, in 1972, had stolen from the museum that employed him a collection of jade pieces that were worth a fortune.

Somewhere, on one of the islands in this particular stretch of river, that fortune now lay buried, exquisite carvings packed in paper inside an old steel suitcase.

"*. . . Because I do not wish they be lost forever, I now write the facts and pray that you may be able to locate them from the description that I give.*"

A letter written and intended for that same museum from which the jade collection had been stolen, but a letter never mailed—perhaps because he never had a chance to mail it, because there was no one to take and mail it for him, not mailed, perhaps, because he had no stamp for the envelope and death was creeping close. Not mailed, but packed away with his other poor possessions in a battered suitcase—a mate, perhaps, to the one in which the jade was buried.

And the suitcase—where had it lain secreted or forgotten ever since the old man died? By what strange route had it finally found its way into that auction house, to be offered on a rainy afternoon along with many other odds and ends? Why had no one ever opened it to see what it might contain? Or might someone have opened it and thought it to be no more than it was—a bunch of junk that had all the appearance of being entirely worthless?

An idle, rainy afternoon, with nothing else to do but seek shelter from the rain. And the mad, illogical, small-boy impulse that had made him start the bidding at a quarter, just for the hell of it, and then no other bids, Hicklin remembered, sitting there and smoking, how he had thought for a moment he should set it down somewhere and then wander off, affecting absentmindedness, leaving it behind, thus getting rid of it. But once again, illogically, he had carried it back to his room and that evening, for lack of anything more interesting to do, had examined its contents and found the letter and been intrigued by it—not believing it, but intrigued enough to make an effort to find out who Steven Furness might have been.

So here he was, beside the river, with the campfire burning and the lament of the whippoorwill sounding from the hollow—the only man in the world who knew (or knew approximately, at least) where the stolen jade lay buried. Perhaps, at this late date, one of the very few who knew about the theft at all.

Even now, he told himself, the jade probably could not be safely placed upon the market. For there would be records still and the museum still existed. But five hundred years from now, a thousand years from now, it could be safely sold. For by then the very fact of the theft would have been forgotten or so deeply buried in the ancient records that it could not be found.

It would make, he told himself, a satisfactory stake for the second life—if he could only find it. Diamonds, he thought, or rubies would be scarcely worth the effort. But jade was different. It would keep its value, as would any work of art. The converters could turn out diamonds by the bushel and they could, in fact, turn out jade as well, by the ton if need be. But they could not turn out carven jade or paintings. Art objects still would retain their value, perhaps appreciate in value. For while the converters could turn out the raw material, any kind of raw material, they could not duplicate a piece of craftsmanship or art.

A man, he told himself, had to use some judgment in selecting what he meant to cache away against Revival Day.

The tobacco had burned out and the pipe made gurgling noises as he sucked at it. He took it from his mouth and tapped out the ash against his boot heel.

Tomorrow morning there'd be fish on the lines that he had set and he still had flour and other makings for a plate of flapjacks. He got up from the ground and went down to the canoe to get his blanket roll.

A good night's sleep and a hearty breakfast and he'd be on his way again—looking for the island with a sandbar at its point shaped somewhat like a fishhook and the two pines just landward of the sandbar. Although, he knew, the sandbar's shape might well have changed or been wiped out entirely. The one hope that he had were the two pine trees, if they still survived.

He stood at the water's edge and glanced up at the sky. The glitter of the stars was unmarred by any cloud and the moon, almost full, hung just above the eastern cliffs. He sniffed the breeze and it was clean and fresh, with a hint of chill in it. Tomorrow, he told himself, would be another perfect day.

16

DANIEL FROST stood on the sidewalk and watched the lights of Ann Harrison's car go down the street until it turned a corner and disappeared from sight.

Then he turned and started up the worn stone steps that led back into the apartment building. But halfway up he hesitated and then turned about and walked down the steps to the street again.

It was too nice a night, he told himself, to go back into his room. But even as he told it to himself, he knew that it was not the beauty of the night, for here, in this ramshackle neighborhood, there was nothing that held any claim to beauty. It was not, he knew, the attractiveness of the night that had turned him back, but a strange reluctance to go back into the room. Wait a while, perhaps, and its emptiness might wear off a little, or his memory might become slightly dulled so that he could accept the emptiness the better.

Until this night he had never known how empty and how drab and colorless and mean that room had been—not until he had come back from the park where he had met Joe Gibbons. And then, for a little time, it had come to a fullness of color, warmth, and beauty with Ann Harrison within the four small walls. There had been some candles and a dozen roses—and the price he'd paid for the roses had seemed to him outrageous—but it was neither the candles nor the roses, nor the both of them together, that had transformed the place. It had been Ann who had brought the miracle.

The room had been mean and empty and it had never been before. It had been simply sensible to live in a place like that, a door for privacy, a roof for shelter, a single window to let in the light and one window was enough. A

73

place for eating and for sleeping, a place to spend his time when he wasn't working. There was no need for larger quarters, no thought of greater comfort. For whatever comfort he might need came from the knowledge that week by week he added to the competence he'd take with him when he died.

Why had the room seemed so mean and small when he'd come back to it that evening? Was it, perhaps, because his life likewise suddenly had become mean and small? That the room was empty because his life was empty? And how could his life be empty when he faced the almost certain prospect of immortality?

The street was in shadow, with only a streetlamp here and there. The rundown structures on each side of the roadway were gaunt specters from the past, old somber residential buildings that long ago had outlived any former pride they may have held.

His footsteps rang like hollow drumbeats on the pavement as he walked slowly down the street. The houses mostly were dark, with only here and there a lighted window. There appeared to be no one else abroad.

No one else abroad, he thought, because there was no reason to go anywhere. No cafes, no plays, no concerts—for all of these took money. And if one were to prepare for that second life, he must hold tight to all his money.

A drab, deserted street and a drab and empty room—was this all that the present life could offer to a man? Could he have been wrong? he wondered. Could he have been walking in a dream, blinded by the glory of the life to come?

All alone, he thought—alone in life and alone upon the street.

Then a man stepped out of a recessed doorway.

"Mr. Frost?" he asked.

"Yes," said Frost. "What can I do for you?"

There was something about the man that he didn't care for, a faint hint of impertinence, a sense of insolence in the way he spoke.

The man moved a step or two closer, but said nothing.

"If you don't mind," said Frost, "I have . . ."

Something stung him in the back of the neck, a vicious, painful sting. He lifted a hand to smite at whatever might have stung him, but his hand was heavy, and half lifted, it would lift no further. He seemed to be falling, over on one side, in a slow, deliberate fall, not from any blow, not from any violence, but as if he'd tried to lean against something that had not been there. And the curious thing about it was that he didn't seem to care, for he knew that he was falling so slowly he'd not be hurt when he struck the sidewalk.

The man who had spoken to him still was standing on the sidewalk, and now there was another man as well, someone, Frost realized, who had come up behind him. But they were faceless men, enshrouded in the shadow of the buildings and they were no one that he knew.

HE was in a dark place and he seemed to be sitting in a chair and in the darkness of the place a light he could not see shone on the metallic structure of a strange machine.

He was comfortable and drowsy, and he felt no desire to move, although it bothered him that he did not recognize the place. It was somewhere, he was certain, he had never been before.

He closed his eyes again and sat there, the hardness of the chair beneath him, across his back and seat, and the hardness of the floor underneath his feet the one reality. He listened and there seemed to be a sort of humming, an almost silent hum, the sort of noise that an idle piece of equipment might make while it waited for a task to be assigned to it.

There was a burning on each cheek and a burning on his forehead, a tingling sensation with a little fire in it and he wondered what had happened and where he was and how he'd gotten there, but he was so comfortable, so very close to sleep, that he didn't really mind.

He sat quietly and now it seemed that in addition to the machinelike hum, he could hear the ticking of time as it went flowing past him. Not the ticking of a clock, for there was no sound of a clock, but the tick of time itself. And that was strange, he thought, for time should have no sound.

Embarrassed by the thought of the tick of time, he stirred a little in the chair and lifted a hand to feel the tingle in his cheek.

"Your Honor," said a voice out of the darkness all around him, "the defendant is awake."

Frost's eyes came open and he struggled to get out of the chair. But his legs seemed to have no power in them and his arms were rubbery and all he really wanted was to stay sitting in the chair.

But the man had said Your Honor and something about a defendant now awake and that was startling enough to make him want to find out where he was.

Another voice asked, "Can he stand?"

"It appears he can't, Your Honor."

"Well," His Honor said, "it doesn't matter much, one way or the other."

Frost managed to hitch around so he was sitting sidewise in the chair and now he saw the light, a little shielded light, on a level somewhat above his head, and just above the light, half in shadow, half in light, hung a ghostly face.

"Daniel Frost," asked the ghostly face, "can you see me?"

"Yes, I can," said Frost.

"Can you hear and understand me?"

"I don't know," said Frost. "It seems I just woke up and I can't get out of the chair . . ."

"You talk too much," said the other voice in the room.

"Leave him be," said the ghostly face. "Give him a little time. This must be a shock to him."

Frost sat limply in the chair and the others waited.

He had been walking on a street, it seemed, when a man had stepped from a doorway and had spoken to him. Then something stung his neck and he'd tried to reach the thing that stung him, but he couldn't reach it. And then he had fallen very slowly, although he could not remember that he'd ever hit the street, and there had been two men, not one, standing on the sidewalk, watching as he fell.

Your Honor, the other man had said, and that must mean a court and if it were a court, the machine would be the Jury, and the place where His Honor sat, with the little shielded light, would be the judge's bench.

But it all was wrong. It was a fantasy. For what reason would he find himself in court?

"You feeling better now?" His Honor asked.

"Yes, I seem to," said Frost, "but there is something wrong. It seems I'm in a courtroom."

"That," said the other voice, "is exactly where you are."

"But there is no reason for me to be in . . ."

"If you'll shut up for a minute," said the other, "His Honor will explain."

When he finished saying it, he snickered and the snicker ran all about the room on little, dirty feet.

"Bailiff," said the face that hung above the bench, "that is the last I want to hear from you. This man is unfortunate, indeed, but he is not a subject for your ridicule."

The other man said nothing.

Frost struggled to his feet, hanging to the chair to hold himself erect.

"I don't know what is going on," he said, "and I have a right to know. I demand . . ."

A ghostly hand waved beside the ghostly head to cut off what he meant to say.

"You have the right," said the face, "and if you'll listen, I'll inform you."

A pair of hands, reaching from behind him, grasped Frost beneath the armpits, hauled him straight, and held him on his feet. Slowly Frost reached out to grasp the back of the chair to hold himself erect.

"I'm quite all right," he said to the man behind him.

The hands released him and he stood alone, propped up by the chair.

"Daniel Frost," said the judge, "I'll make this brief and to the point. There is no other way.

"You have been seized and brought to this court and have undergone a narco-trial. You have been found guilty of the charge and sentence already has been passed and executed, according to the law."

"But that's ridiculous," Frost cried out. "What have I done? What was the charge?"

"Treason," said the judge.

"Treason. Your Honor, you are crazy. How could I . . ."

"Not treason to the state. Treason to humanity."

Frost stood rigid, his hands gripping the wood of the chair so hard that the grasp was painful. A tumult of fear went surging through him and his brain seemed curdled. Words came churning up, but he did not say them. He kept his mouth clamped shut.

For this was not the time, said one tiny corner of his mind that still stayed sane, for the rush of words, for an outpouring of emotion. Perhaps he already had said more than he should have. Words were tools and must be used to their best advantage.

"Your Honor," he finally said, "I challenge you on that. There is no provision . . ."

"But there is," said the judge. "Think of it and you'd realize that there had to be. There has to be provision against the sabotage of the plan to prolong human life. I can quote you . . ."

Frost shook his head. "No need to, although I've never heard of it. But even so, there has been no treason on my part. I've worked for that very plan; I've worked for Forever Center . . ."

"Under narco-questioning," said the judge, "you admitted to conniving with various publishers, using your position, for motives of your own, to prejudice the plan."

"It's a lie!" yelled Frost. "That was not the way it was." The ghostly head shook slowly, sadly.

"It must have been the way it was. You told of it yourself. You testified against yourself. You would not lie about yourself and to your discredit."

"A trial!" Frost said bitterly. "In the middle of the night. Struck down in the street and carried here. No arrest. No attorney. And, I would suppose, no chance to appeal."

"You are right," said the judge. "There is no appeal. Under law, narco-trial results and judgments stand final. After all, it is the most equable approach to justice. It does away with all impediments to the course of justice."

"Justice!"

"Mr. Frost," said the judge, "I have been patient with you. Because of your former position of trust and honor and your long record with Forever Center, I have given you more latitude in your remarks than conforms with the dignity of this court. I can assure you that the trial was conducted properly and by the only means that a trial for treason can be conducted under law, that you have been found guilty of the charge and that sentence has been passed. I now will read the sentence to you."

A phantom hand reached into the darkness where a pocket was and, bringing out a pair of spectacles, placed them on the ghostly face. The seemingly detached hand picked up a sheaf of papers and the papers rustled.

"Daniel Frost," said the judge, reading from the paper, "you have been adjudged, after due legal process, guilty of the charge of treason against all humankind in that you attempted willingly and willfully to obstruct the administrative functions and processes aimed at the bringing of immortality not only to all presently living persons but to all the others who are dead, with their bodies held in preservation.

"It is the sentence of this court, in accordance with the penalty set out by the statutes, that you, Daniel Frost, shall be ostracized from the human race, that you shall be forbidden . . ."

"No!" yelled Frost. "No, you can't do that to me. I didn't . . ."

"Bailiff," roared the judge.

A hand reached out of the darkness and the fingers ground into Frost's shoulder.

"You shut up," said the bailiff, grinding his teeth, "and listen to His Honor."

". . . that you shall be forbidden," the judge went on, "to have any intercourse, commerce, or communication, in any manner whatsoever, with any other member of the human race, and that any other member of the human race, under duly set forth penalties, shall be forbidden to have any intercourse, commerce, or communication with you. That you shall have stripped from you all personal possessions except, for the sake of decency, the very clothes you stand in, and that all other of your possessions shall be confiscated. Likewise you are stripped of all rights except the one final right of having your body preserved, in accordance with the law, and by the mercy of this court.

"And it is hereby directed that, in order all men may recognize your ostracism and so refrain from any contact with you, you be branded, by the means of a tattoo, upon your forehead and each cheek with an O outlined in red."

The judge laid down the paper and took off his glasses.

"I have one thing to add," he said. "As a matter of mercy, the tattooing already has been done, while you still were under drug. It is a rather painful process and it is not the purpose of this court to cause you unnecessary agony or greater humiliation than is unavoidable.

"And a warning. The court is aware that by various means these tattoo marks may be covered or disguised, or even removed. Do not, under any circumstance, be tempted to resort to such deception. The penalty for such an act is the cancellation of the one right you still have left, the preservation of your body."

He glared at Frost. "Sir," he asked, "do you understand?"

"Yes," Frost mumbled. "Yes, I understand."

The judge reached for his gavel and banged it. The sound rang hollowly in the almost-empty room.

"This case is closed," he said. "Bailiff, escort him to the street and throw him—I mean, turn him loose."

18

IN the night, the cross blew down again.

19

THE faint lighting of the eastern sky served notice that dawn was near at hand.

Daniel Frost stood unsteadily in the street, still numb from the impact of what had happened in the courtroom, still held in the dying grip of drug, filled with a strange blend of desperation, of anger, fear, and pity for himself.

There was something very wrong about all of it, he knew—not only the fact that he could not have been convicted as they had said he'd been convicted, but wrong about the hour, a trial in the dead of night, and in the fact that there had been no other persons in the court but the judge and bailiff. If in fact they had been judge and bailiff.

A put-up job, he thought. The long arm of Marcus Appleton reaching out for him. And reaching out most desperately. There must, he told himself, be something in that paper that Appleton would go to any lengths to hide.

But he was in no position at the moment—if he ever were to be in position—to do anything about it. There was no one who would listen to him. There was no one he would dare to talk with. There is no appeal, the ghostly face had said. And that was right; there was no way to appeal.

Ann Harrison, he thought.

Good Lord, there was Ann Harrison.

Had she been the trigger, her coming up to see him, that had brought this all about?

And had he said anything about her? Had he said she had the paper—if she really had the paper?

If he had been questioned under drug, he undoubtedly had implicated her. But it seemed impossible to believe that he had been so questioned, for if he had (and the court had really been a duly constituted court) he'd not have been convicted.

He stood shaky in the night just before the dawn and the questions and the doubts and the fumbling for an understanding went on roaring through his brain.

No longer a member of the human race.

No longer anything.

Just a blob of protoplasm tossed out in the street—naked of possessions and of hope.

With but one single right remaining—the human right to die.

And that, of course, was what Appleton had planned.

That was what he counted on—that with no other right, a man would exercise that one remaining right.

"I won't do it, Marcus," said Daniel Frost, talking to himself and to the night and to the world and to Marcus Appleton.

He turned from where he stood and went fumbling down the street, for he had to get away, before the light could come he must find a place to hide. To hide from the mockery and the anger and the callous cruelty that would greet him if he should happen to be seen. For now he was no longer of the world, but an enemy. Every hand would be raised against him and he'd have no protection beyond the protection of the dark and hidden place. He was, henceforth, his own protector, for there was no law nor right that he could claim.

Within him grew a cold hard knot of anger and of viciousness that wiped out the self-pity that remained. A knot of hard, cold anger that such a thing as had happened to him could be allowed to happen. It was not civilized—but who had ever claimed that the human race was civilized? It could probe through the cosmos for other earthlike planets, it could pry at the lid of time, it could conquer death and aim at eternal life, but it was still a tribe.

There had to be a way to beat this vicious tribe, there had to be a way to square accounts with Appleton—and if there were a way he would seek it out and use it and use it without pity.

But not right now.

Right now he must find a place to hide.

He would be all right, he knew, being honest with himself, so long as he was able to hang onto that knot of anger which twisted in his belly. The one thing that he must never do was to give way to a slobbering pity of himself.

He reached an intersection and hesitated, wondering which way he should go. From far off, somewhere on another street, came the thin whining of an electric motor—a cruising cab, perhaps.

To the river, he thought—that would be the place where he would be most likely to find a place where he could hide, perhaps even get some sleep if he could manage sleep. And after that, he told himself, would come the problem of locating food.

He shivered, thinking of it. Was this what life was to be from this moment forward—a seeking of a place to hide and sleep, the eternal hunt for food? In a little while, with the threat of winter, he'd have to start drifting south, wandering (at night, when he'd be unobserved) down through that great complex of coastal cities which really was one city.

The light was growing in the east and he must be on his way. But he felt a strange reluctance to turn in the direction of the river. He wasn't really running yet and he didn't want to run—except for the tattoos on his face there was no reason that he should. But the first step that he took toward the river, he would be in flight, and he shrank from flight, for it seemed that once he took that first step he'd never stop his running.

He stood looking up and down the empty street. There might be some other way, he thought. Perhaps he should not even try to hide. There must be someplace where he could demand the justice that was coming to him, but even as he thought of it he knew what the answer would be: That he had had his justice.

It was a ridiculous thing to think about, he knew. He had no chance at all. He would not be heard. The evidence of his status and his crime was upon his face for everyone to see. And he had no rights.

Wearily he turned in the direction of the river. If he had to run, he'd better start the running before it was too late.

A voice spoke to him: "Daniel Frost."

He spun around.

A man who apparently had been standing in the shadow at the base of the building on the corner stepped out onto the sidewalk—a hunched, misshapen figure with a large cap squashed flat upon his head and with tatters hanging from his coat sleeves.

"No," said Frost, uncertainly. "No . . ."

"It's all right, Mr. Frost. You're to come with me."

"But," said Frost, "you don't know what I am. You don't understand."

"Of course we do," said the man with the tattered sleeves. "We know that you need help and that is all that matters. Please stay very close behind me."

20

DESPITE the lighted lantern, the place was dark. The lantern cast no more than a shallow puddle of illumination and the humped shapes of the people in the room were simply darker shadows in the dark vastness they inhabited.

Frost halted and in the dark he felt the impact of eyes he knew were watching him.

Friend or foe? he wondered—although out on the street (how many blocks from here?) the man who'd been his guide had indicated friend. You need help, he'd said, and that is all that matters.

The man who'd guided him walked forward toward the group seated by the lantern. Frost stayed where he was. His feet hurt from all the walking and he was tired clear through and the effects of the drug, he thought, might not have entirely worn off. The needle, or the dart, or whatever it had been that had struck him in the neck must have been really loaded.

He watched the guide squat down and whisper with the others seated by the lantern and he wondered where he was. It was somewhere on the waterfront, for his nose had told him that much, and probably was a cellar or a basement, because they had gone down several flights of stairs before they had arrived. A hideout of some sort, he guessed, the very kind of place he would have hunted on his own.

"Mr. Frost," said an old-man voice, "why don't you come over here and sit down with us. I suspect that you are tired."

Frost stumbled forward and sat down on the floor near the lantern and the voice. His eyes were becoming somewhat accustomed to the darkness and now the humps were human and the faces were white blurs.

"I thank you, sir," he said. "I am a little tired."

"You had a bitter night," said the man.

Frost nodded.

"Leo tells me you've been ostracized."

"I'll leave if you want me to," said Frost. "Just let me rest a little."

"There is no need of that," said the man. "You now are one of us. We all are ostracized."

Frost jerked up his head and stared at the man who spoke. He had a grizzled face, the jowls and chin shining with a two-day stubble of white whiskers.

"I don't mean we wear the mark," the old man said. "But we still are ostracized. We are non-conformists and today you cannot afford to fail to conform. We don't believe, you see. Or, perhaps, on the other hand, you might say that we believe too much. But in the wrong things, naturally."

"I don't understand," said Frost.

The old man chuckled. "It is clear to see you don't know where you are."

"Of course I don't," Frost said testily, impatient with this baiting. "I have not been told."

"You're in a den of Holies," said the man. "Take a good look at us. We are those dirty and unthinking people who go out at night and paint the signs on walls. We are the ones who preach on street corners and in parks, we are the ones who hand out all those filthy and non-Forever tracts. That is, until the cops come and run us all away."

"Look," Frost said, wearily, "I don't mind who you are. I am grateful to you for taking me in, for if you hadn't, I don't know what I'd have done. I was about to look for a place to hide, for I knew I had to hide, but I didn't know how to go about it. And then this man came along and . . ."

"An innocent," said the old man. "A sheltered innocent thrown out in the street. Of course you wouldn't have known what to do. You'd have gotten into all sorts of trouble. But there really was no need to worry. We've been watching over you."

"Watching over me? Why should you do that?"

"Rumors," said the man. "There were all sorts of rumors. And we hear all the rumors that there are. We make it our business to hear every sort of rumor and to sort them out."

"Let me guess," said Frost. "The rumor said someone was out to get me."

"Yes. Because you knew too much. About something, incidentally, we could not determine."

"You must," said Frost, "watch over many people."

"Not so many," said the grizzled man. "Although we keep well informed about Forever Center. We have some pipelines there."

I bet you do, thought Frost. For somehow, despite his rescue, he didn't like this man.

"But you are tired," said the man, "and likely also hungry."

He rose and clapped his hands. Somewhere a door came open and a shaft of light spread into the room.

"Food," said the man, speaking to the woman who stood in the crack of doorway. "Some food for our guest."

The door closed and the man sat down again, this time close to Frost, almost side by side with him.

The odor of an unwashed body poured out from him. He held his hands limply in his lap and Frost could see that the hands were grimy, the nails untrimmed and with heavy dirt embedded underneath them.

"I would imagine," said the man, "that you may be somewhat chagrined in finding yourself with us. I wish however, you would not feel that way. We really are good-hearted people. We may be dissenters and protestants, but we have a right to make our voice heard in any way we can."

Frost nodded. "Yes, of course, you have. But it seems to me there might have been better ways for you to get a hearing. You've been at it for—how long has it been, fifty years or more?"

"And we haven't gotten very far. That's the point you wish to make?"

"I suppose it is," said Frost.

"We know, of course," said the other, "that we will not win. There is no way of winning. But our conscience tells us that we must bear witness. So long as we can continue to make our feeble voice heard in the wilderness, we will not have failed."

Frost said nothing. He felt his body sinking into a comfortable lethargy and he had no wish to try to pull it out.

The man reached out a dirty hand and laid it on Frost's knee.

"You read the Bible, son?"

"Yes, off and on. I've read most of it."

"And why did you read it?"

"Why, I don't know," said Frost, startled at the question. "Because it's a human document. Perhaps in hope of some spiritual comfort, although I can't be sure of that. Because, I suppose, in many ways, it is good literature."

"But without conviction?"

"I suppose you're right. Without any great conviction."

"There was a time when many people read it with devout conviction. There was a day when it was a light shining in the darkness of the soul. Not too long ago it was life and hope and promise. And now the best that you can say of it is that it's good literature.

"It's your talk of physical immortality that has brought all this about. Why should people read the Bible any more or believe in it or believe in anything at all if they have the legal—not the spiritual, mind you, but the legal—promise of immortality? And how can you promise immortality? Immortality means going on forever and forever and no one can promise that, no mortal man can promise forever and forever."

"You're mistaken," said Frost. "I have not promised it."

"I'm sorry. I speak too generally. Not you, personally, of course. But Forever Center."

"Not entirely Forever Center, either," said Frost. "Rather man himself. If there had been no Forever Center, man still would have sought immortality. It is a thing that, in the very nature of him, he could not have ignored. It's not in man's nature to do less than he can. He may fail, of course, but he'll always try."

"It's the devil in him," said the grizzled man. "The forces of darkness and corruption work in many ways to thwart man's inherent godliness."

Frost said: "Please, I don't want to argue with you. Some other time, perhaps. But not right now. You must understand that I am grateful to you, and . . ."

"Would anyone else in all this land," the man demanded, "have held out a hand of fellowship to you at a moment such as this?"

Frost shook his head. "No, I don't imagine there is anyone who would."

"But we did," said the man. "We, the humble ones. We, the true believers."

"Yes," said Frost, "I give you that. You did."

"And you don't ask yourself why we may have done it?"

"Not yet," said Frost, "but I suppose I will."

"We did it," said the man, "because we value not the man, not the mortal body, but the soul. You read in old historical writings that a nation numbers not so many people, but so many souls. And this may seem quaint and strange to you, but those old writings are a reflection of how men thought in those days, when the human animal always was aware of God and of the life hereafter and was less concerned with worldliness and the present moment."

The door came open and the light streamed out into the room again. An old and wrinkled woman moved into the range of the lantern light. She carried in her hand a bowl and half a loaf of bread and these she handed to the grizzled man.

"Thank you, Mary," said the man, and the woman backed away.

"Food," said the man, putting down the bowl in front of Frost and handing him the bread.

"I thank you very much," said Frost.

He lifted the spoon that was in the bowl and carried a spoonful of the substance to his mouth. It was soup, weak and watery.

"And now I understand," said the grizzled man, "that in just a few more years a man need not even go through the ritual of death to attain immortality. Once Forever Center has this immortality business all written down and the methods all worked out, a man will be made immortal out of hand. He'll just stay young and go on living and there won't be any death. Once you get born, then you will live forever."

"It won't be," said Frost, "for a few years yet."

"But once it can be done, that will be the way of it?"

"I suppose it will," said Frost. "Once you have it it's just plain foolishness to let a man grow old and die before you give him eternal youth and life."

"Oh, the vanity of it," the old man wailed. "The terrible waste of it. The impertinence!"

Frost did not answer him. There wasn't much of an answer, actually, to be given. He simply went on eating.

The man nudged him in the arm. "One thing more, son. Do you believe in God?"

Slowly Frost put the spoon back into the bowl.

He asked: "You really want an answer?"

"I want an answer," said the man. "I want an honest one."

"The answer," said Frost, "is that I don't know. Not, certainly, in the kind of God that you are thinking of. Not the old white-whiskered, woodcut gentleman. But a supreme being—yes, I would believe in a God of that sort. Because it seems to me there must be some sort of force or power or will throughout the universe. The universe is too orderly for it to be otherwise. When you measure all this orderliness, from the mechanism of the atom at one end of the scale, out to the precision of the operation of the universe at the other end, it seems unbelievable that there is not a supervisory force of some kind, a benevolent ruling force to maintain that sort of order."

"Order!" the man exploded. "All you talk about is order! Not holiness, not godliness . . ."

"I'm sorry," Frost said. "You asked for an honest answer. I gave you an honest one. Please take my word for it—I would give a lot to have the kind of faith you have, blind, unquestioning faith without a single doubt. But even then I wonder if faith would be enough."

"Faith is all man has," the man told him. quietly.

"You take faith," Frost said, "and make a virtue of it. A virtue of not knowing . . ."

"If we knew," the man said, positively, "there would be no faith. And we need the faith."

Somewhere someone was shouting and there was the far-off sound of feet pounding rapidly.

The grizzled man rose quickly and in the act of rising one of his feet stepped sidewise and caught the bowl of soup and overturned it. In the light of the lantern, it ran like slow oil across the floor.

"The cops!" someone shouted and everyone was moving very rapidly. Someone grasped the lantern and lifted it and the flame went out. The room was plunged in darkness.

Frost had risen, too. He took a step and someone bumped

into him, driving him backward in an awkward stumble. And then he felt the floor give way beneath his feet with the faint popping and snapping of long-rotten boards and he was plunging downward. He threw out his arms instinctively, clutching for any support that he might find. The fingers of his left hand closed upon the end of a broken board, but even as he grasped it, the weight of his falling body snapped it and he was through the floor and falling.

His body landed with a splash and evil-smelling water rose in a sheet and slapped him in the face.

The fall had thrown him forward and now he raised himself so that he squatted in the foulness that was all about him—the darkness and the foulness a part of one another.

He twisted about and glanced up and he could not see the hole through which he'd fallen, but from the floor above him came the thud of running feet and the sound of distant voices, drawing rapidly away.

New thuddings came and new voices, very sharp and angry, and the splintering of boards as someone broke a door. Feet pounded once again on the floor above him and thin beams of light danced across the hole where he had fallen.

Fearful that someone would flash a light directly down the hole and catch him in its beam, he moved slowly forward, water swirling at his ankles.

The feet pounded back and forth and ran into far rooms and returned again and snatches of voices floated down to him.

"Got away again," one voice said. "Someone tipped them off."

"Pretty dismal," said another. "Just the kind of place you would expect . . ."

And then another voice, and at the sound of it, Frost stiffened and took another involuntary step farther from the hole in the floor above.

"Men," said the voice of Marcus Appleton, "we missed them once again. There'll be another day."

Other voices answered, but the words were indistinct.

"I'll get those sons of bitches," said Marcus Appleton, "if it's the last thing that I do."

The voices and the footsteps moved away and in a little time were gone.

Silence fell, broken only by the slow drip of water falling from some place into the pool in which Frost stood.

A tunnel of some sort, he guessed. Or perhaps a sub-basement flooded by seepage from the river.

Now the problem was to get out of here. Although without a light of any sort that might not be easy. And the one way to do it was to try to get out the way he had come in, through the hole in the floor above.

He reached above his head and his fingers touched the rough surface of a beam. He stood on tiptoe and stretched and he could touch the floor above. But he would have to move slowly and try to maintain some sort of orientation, for the place was in utter darkness and his fingers were his eyes.

Slowly he worked his way along and finally found the hole. Now, he'd have to jump for it and grab hold of the rotten boards and hope that they would support his weight so he could pull himself into the room above. Once there, he told himself, he'd be safe for a time at least, for Appleton and his men would not be coming back. Neither would the Holies. He would be on his own.

He stood for a moment to catch his breath and suddenly, from all around him rose a squeaking and a scurrying, the rush of tiny feet, the slithering of bodies rushing through the dark, and the angry squealing of ravening creatures driven by a desperate hunger.

His scalp tightened and it seemed that his hair rose upon his head.

Rats! Rats rushing at him through the dark!

Fear powered his muscles and he leaped, driving himself chest high through the hole. Scrambling and kicking, he pulled himself clear and lay panting on the floor.

Underneath him the squeaking and the squealing rose in a wave, then slowly died away.

Frost still lay upon the floor and after a time the trembling stopped and the sweat dried on his body and he got to his hands and knees and crawled until he found a corner and there he huddled against the terror and the loneliness of the new life that he faced.

21

GODFREY CARTWRIGHT leaned far back in his padded chair and clasped his hands behind his head. It was the position he assumed when he was about to discuss some weighty matters, but wanted to seem casual in his discussion of them.

"The way I see it," he said, "something queered the deal. No publisher before ever offered the kind of money that I did, and even a stuffed shirt like Frost would have grabbed it if he thought he had a chance of not getting caught at it. But now Frost has disappeared and Joe Gibbons is nowhere to be found. Maybe Appleton had a hand in it. It would have to be someone like Appleton, for there are just a few in Forever Center who know that censorship is being carried on. And if Appleton found out, he's not a man to fool with."

"You mean," said Harris Hastings, plaintively, "that you won't put out my book."

Cartwright stared at him. "Why, bless you, man," he said, "we never said we would."

Hastings squirmed in his chair. He was an unprepossessing sight. His head was round and hairless, looking somewhat like a naked sphere with a face upon it. He wore thick glasses and he squinted. His billiard-ball head rode thrust forward on his shoulders and this, tied in with the squint, gave him the appearance of a man who was more than a bit befuddled, but trying very hard to understand.

"But you said . . ."

"I said," Cartwright told him, "that I thought your book would sell. I said that if it could be published we'd make a mint of money on it. But I also told you that I had to be sure, before any more was done, that we could get it before the public. I didn't want to run the chance of Frost finding out about it when we had a lot of money in it and then bringing pressure on us. Once we had it published and up for sale, why, then, of course, Frost couldn't do a thing, for if he tried there'd be a public uproar and a public uproar is the one thing Forever Center doesn't want."

"But you told me . . ." Hastings said again.

"I told you, sure," said Cartwright, "but we haven't got a contract and the deal is dead. I told you I couldn't give you one until I saw if I could make a deal with Frost. I couldn't take the chance. Frost had a lot of snoopers and I can tell you they were good. Joe Gibbons is one of the best of them and Joe has always made a sort of specialty of us and some half dozen other houses. He kept close tab on us; he had pipelines into us. I don't know who it was. If I had known I'd have canned them long ago. But the point is that we couldn't have made a move without Joe finding out about it and he did find out about it, just the way I knew he would. The only thing that I could do was try to make a deal. I don't mind telling you that your book was one of the few I ever tried to make a deal to publish."

"But the work," Hastings said, in anguish. "The work I put into it. I put twenty years in it. Do you realize what twenty years of research and writing means? I put my life into it, I tell you. I made a life of it. I sold my life for it."

Cartwright said, easily, "You believe it, don't you—this stuff you wrote."

"Of course I believe it," Hastings exploded. "Can't you see that it's the truth? I searched the records and I know it is the truth. The circumstantial evidence is there for anyone to see. This plan, this life continuation, this whatever you may call it, is the greatest hoax that ever has been played upon the human race. Its purpose was not, it never was, what it purports to be. It was, instead, a last and desperate measure to bring an end to war. For if you could make people believe that their bodies could be preserved and later be revived, who would go to war—what man would fight in any war? What government or nation would dare become involved in war? For the victims of a war could not hope for preservation of their bodies. In many cases there'd be very little of the bodies to preserve. In cases where there was, facilities for the retrieval and preservation of those bodies could not operate.

"And it may be that the ends justified the means. It may

be that we cannot condemn the trickery. For war was a terrible thing. We today, who have not known war for more than a century, cannot know how terrible. There was actual fear, a hundred years ago, that another major war might wipe out all human culture, if not all life, from earth. And in the light of this the hoax may be justified. But in any case, the people should be told, they should be . . ."

He stopped and looked at Cartwright, still propped back in his chair, with his hands behind his head.

"You don't believe any of this, do you?"

The publisher took his hands from behind his head and sat forward in the chair, leaning his forearms on the desk top.

"Harris," he said, earnestly, "it doesn't matter whether I believe or not. It's not my business to believe in the books I publish, beyond the one belief that they will make some money. I'd like to publish your book because I know that it would sell. You can't expect more of me than that."

"But now you say you won't publish it."

Cartwright nodded. "That is right. Not won't, but can't. Forever Center wouldn't let me."

"They couldn't stop you."

"No, not legally. But there can be pressure brought—not only on myself but on the stockholders and the other officers of this company. And you must not forget that Forever Center itself owns some of the stock, as it owns a part, or all, of everything upon the entire earth. The pressure that they could bring would be unbelievable if you hadn't seen it. As I said, if I could have got it published and on sale, then I'd have been in the clear. It would have been Frost's error then, not mine. His neck, not mine. It would have been something that he should have caught, but didn't, something that he slipped up on. The onus of the entire thing would have been shifted off my shoulders. The only thing they could have charged me with was a piece of bad judgment, and perhaps poor taste, and that I could have stood. But the way it is . . ."

He made a hopeless gesture.

"I could try other publishers."

"Sure you could," said Cartwright.

"By that I suppose you mean none of them would touch it either."

"Not with a ten-foot pole. By now the news is out—that I tried to buy off Frost and failed and now Frost is among the missing. Every publisher in town has heard about it. There are all sorts of whispers flying."

"Then it'll never be published."

"I'm afraid you're right. Just go home and sit down in a chair and feel smug and comfortable that you've uncovered something that is too big for anyone to touch, that you're the only man who knows the secret, that you were astute enough to uncover a plot that no one, absolutely no one, ever had suspected."

Hastings hunched his head even farther forward.

"There is a trace of mockery in your words," he said, "that I'm not too sure I like. Tell me, if you will, what your version is."

"My version?"

"Yes. What do you really think about Forever Center?"

"Why," asked Cartwright, "what's so wrong in thinking that it's exactly the way they say it is?"

"Nothing, I suppose. It's the comfortable viewpoint for one to take, but it isn't true."

"Most people think it is. There's talk, of course, and rumors—you hear them everywhere. But I think most people take the talk and rumors for sheer entertainment. They talk about it and listen to it, but they really don't believe it. There's so little entertainment these days that people hang onto all that they can get. Go and read about the entertainment of two hundred years ago, or even less than that. The night life in the cities, the theater, the opera, the music. And there were sports—baseball and football and a lot of other things. And where are they all now? Strangled to death by the miserly leanings of our present culture. Pay to see a show when you can stay at home and watch TV? Hell, no! Pay to get into a ball game? Who wants to see a ball game when he can buy a share of Forever stock with what the ticket would cost? Pay fancy prices to get some entertainment when you eat? Are you crazy? When you go out to eat now, and not too many do, you go out to eat and nothing else—no frills. That's why books sell as well as they do. We keep them cheap—shoddy, but cheap. When you're through reading a book someone else can read it and after a while you can read it again yourself. But a ball game or a show, you could only see it once. That's why people are newspaper readers and book readers and TV watchers. They can get a lot of entertainment for almost next to nothing. Cheap entertainment, and much of it's cheap, believe me, but it fills up the hours. Hell, that's all we're doing—filling up the hours. Grabbing everything we can and filling up the hours, aiming everything at our second shot at life. That explains the rumors and the stories and the talk. All of it is free and the people suck it dry, get everything they can get out of it before they turn it loose."

"You," said Hastings, "should write a book, yourself."

"I may," said Cartwright, contentedly. "By God, I really may. Take the hide off them and their penny-pinching lives. They'd eat it up. They'd like it. Give them stuff to talk about for months."

"You think, then, that my book . . ."

"That's one," said Cartwright, "that some of them might actually have believed in. You have it all annotated and doumented within an inch of its very life. Impressive sort of stuff. I don't see how you did it."

"You still don't believe it," said the author, bitterly. "You have a sneaking hunch I faked it."

"Well, now," said Cartwright, "you can't say I said that. I never asked you, did I?"

He stared off into space, with a lost look on his face.

"Too bad," he said. "Too bad. We could have made a billion. I tell you, boy, no kidding, we could have made a billion."

22

CROUCHED in the alley, behind a pile of weather-beaten boxes that had been thrown there long ago by some small establishment which fronted on the narrow, dingy street— thrown and forgotten and never removed—Frost waited until the man came out of the back door of the hole-in-the-wall eating place and put the garbage into the cans that stood against the wall.

And when he finally came, he carried, as well as the basket full of garbage, a bundle, wrapped in newspaper, which he placed on the ground beside the cans. Then he took the lids off the cans and lifted the bundles of garbage from the heavy basket in which he carried them and put them in the cans. Having done this, he picked up the bundle he had placed beside the cans and balanced it on the lid of one of the cans. For a moment he stood, looking up and down the alley, a white-smudged figure in the darkness, outlined by the feeble glow that invaded the alley from the street. Then he picked up the basket and went back into the restaurant.

Frost rose and, moving swiftly, picked up the bundle off the can. He tucked it underneath his arm and retreated down the alley, stopping at the alley's mouth. There were a few people on the street and he waited until they had moved a bit away, then darted quickly across the street into the opposite alley.

Five blocks away, following the successive alleys, he came to the rear of a dilapidated building, small and with half the roof torn off it, as if someone at one time had started to raze it and then had figured it wasn't worth the trouble. Now it stood, sad and sagging and abandoned, just a little farther along the road to ruin than its fellows on either side of it.

100

A stairs built of stone, with a bent and rusted guardrail leading from its top, ran down into the basement.

Ducking swiftly from the alley, Frost went down the stairs. At the bottom a door, still held upright by one rusted hinge, stood propped against the jamb. By some tugging and hauling, Frost got it open, went through it into the basement, then shoved it shut again.

Having done that, he was home—a home that he had found ten days before, after a long succession of other hiding places that had been worse by far than this. For the basement was cool and dry and it had no rats or no other vermin in too noticeable a number and it seemed to be safe and forgotten, perhaps safe because it was forgotten. No one ever came around.

"Hello there," said someone from the dark.

Frost spun on his heels, crouching as he spun, dropping the bundle to the floor.

"Don't worry," said the voice. "I know who you are and I won't cause you any trouble."

Frost did not move. He held his crouch. Hope and fear wrestled in his brain. One of the Holies who had sought him out again? Someone from Forever Center? Perhaps a man sent by Marcus Appleton?

"How did you track me down?" he whispered.

"I've been looking for you. I have been asking around. Someone saw you in the alley. You are Frost, aren't you?"

"Yes, I'm Frost."

The man came out of the gloom in which he stood. The half-light from a basement window showed the human shape of him, but little else.

"I am glad I found you, Frost," he said. "My name is Franklin Chapman."

"Chapman? Wait a minute! Franklin Chapman is the man . . ."

"Right," the other said. "Ann Harrison talked with you about me."

Frost felt the wild laughter rising in him and sought to choke it down, but it rose in spite of him and sputtered through his lips. He sat down limply on the floor and let his hands hang helplessly, while he shook with the bitter laughter that came flooding up in him.

101

"My God," he said, gasping, "you are the man—you are the one I promised I would help!"

"Yes," said Chapman. "At times, events turn out to be rather strange."

Slowly the laughter died away, but Frost still sat limp and weak.

"I'm glad you came," he finally said, "although I can't imagine why you did."

"Ann sent me. She asked if I'd try to find you. She found out what happened to you."

"Found out? It should have been in the papers. All a reporter had to do was look up the record."

"That's what she did, of course. And it was there, all right, but no word in the papers. Not a single line. But all sorts of rumors. The town is full of rumors."

"What kind of rumors?"

"A scandal of some sort at Center. You've disappeared and Center is trying to hush it up."

Frost nodded. "It figures. Papers tipped off to shut their eyes and rumors started to make it seem that I ran away. Do you think Center knows where I am?"

"I don't know," said Chapman. "I picked up a lot of talk while I looked for you. I'm not the only one who has been asking questions."

"It didn't work the way they thought it would. They thought that after a day or two I'd go and apply for death."

"Most men would have."

"Not me," said Frost. "I've had a lot of time to do my thinking. I always can go down to the vaults. As a last desperate measure, when I can't stand it any longer, that is always left. But not yet. Not for a while."

He hesitated, then spoke again. "I'm sorry, Chapman. I didn't think. I shouldn't talk this way."

"It doesn't bother me," said Chapman. "Not any more. Not now that the shock is over. After all, I'm no worse off than many men before me. I've gotten sort of used to it. I try not to think about it too much."

"You've spent a lot of time hunting me. How about your job?"

"They fired me. I knew they would."

"I'm sorry."

"Oh, it worked out all right. I've got a TV contract and

a publisher is paying someone else to write a book. Wanted me to write it myself, but I told him I couldn't get the words down."

"The dirty creeps," said Frost. "Anything to sell the suckers."

"I know," said Chapman, "but I don't mind. I know what they are doing and it's all right with me. I have a family that has to be raised and a wife who should have something laid away before she dies. It's the least I can do for her. I made them pay. I turned them down to start with and then when they kept after me I named a figure I thought they wouldn't touch, but they did, and I am satisfied. The old lady will have plenty laid away."

Frost got up from the floor, searched for his bundle and found it.

"Man up the street, fellow at a restaurant, puts it out for me each night. I don't know who he is."
old, all wizened up. Said he saw you going through the

"I talked with him," said Chapman. "Little scrawny man, garbage cans. Didn't think anyone should have to get his eats that way."

"Let's go over here and sit down," suggested Frost. "There's an old davenport that someone left down here. I sleep on it. Springs busted and pretty badly beaten up, but it's better than the floor."

Chapman followed him and the two sat down together.

"How bad has it been?" asked Chapman.

"Bad to start with," Frost told him. "Some Holies snatched me off the street, saved my life, more than likely. Talked with a crazy old bastard who asked me if I read the Bible and believed in God. Then Appleton and a bunch of his hoodlums raided the place. Appleton has been trying to catch some of the Holies' ringleaders. I figure the old buzzard I talked with was one of them. I fell through a rotten place in the floor and when they left I crawled out again. Stayed there for a couple of days because I was scared to go out, but I finally got so hungry that I had to go. You ever imagine what it would be like finding food in a city where you couldn't beg for it and didn't dare to steal it, when you couldn't talk with anyone, when you didn't want to talk with anyone because you might get them into trouble if you did?"

"I never thought about it," Chapman said. "I can imagine what it's like."

"There wasn't anything but the garbage cans. It takes a lot, believe me, to eat something out of a garbage can. The first time, that is. When you get hungry enough, you can manage it. After a day or two, you become something of a garbage connoisseur. And a place to hide, a place to sleep —they aren't easy to find and you have to keep changing around, can't stay in one place too long. People see you and get curious. I've stayed here longer than I should because this is the best I've found. That's why you were able to track me down. If I'd changed around, you wouldn't have found me.

"My beard is growing—no razor, you know. And so is my hair. In a little while the beard will cover the tattoos on my cheeks and I can push the hair down to cover the forehead. Once the hair and beard grow long enough maybe I can even venture out in daylight. Still won't dare to talk with anyone, have anything to do with anyone, but won't have to hide so much. People may stare at me, although maybe not so much, for there are some weird characters down in this area. Haven't had anything to do with them. Afraid to. You have to feel your way along, get the hang of this sort of life."

He stopped and stared in the darkness at the white blur of Chapman's face.

"Sorry," he said, tersely, "I talk too much. A man gets hungry for it."

"Go ahead," said Chapman. "I'll sit and listen. Ann will want to know how you are."

"That's another thing," said Frost. "I don't want her getting involved in this business. Tell her to keep out of it. She can't help me and she'll end up getting hurt. Tell her to forget about me."

"She won't do that," Chapman told him. "And I won't, either. You were the only man who was willing to go to bat for me."

"I didn't do a thing for you. I couldn't do a thing for you. It was just a four-flushing gesture. I knew at the time I couldn't help you."

"Mister," said Chapman, "that doesn't make a bit of difference. No matter what you could have done, you were willing to commit yourself. You won't get me to forget it."

"Well, then, do me a favor. You and Ann, too. Keep away from me. Don't get messed up with me. I don't want you to get hurt and if you keep fooling around, you will. There is no one who can be of any help. If it ever gets too bad, I have an easy out."

"I won't let you cut yourself off entirely," insisted Chapman. "Let's make a deal. I won't try to contact you again, but if you ever need anything, any kind of help, let's set up a place where you can find me."

"I won't come for help," said Frost, "but if it'll make you feel any better . . ."

"You'll be staying around this neighborhood?"

"I doubt it. But I can always come back to it."

"About three blocks from here there's a small neighborhood library. And a bench in front of it."

"I know the place," said Frost.

"I'll be there every evening between nine and ten, say on Wednesdays and Saturdays."

"That's too much trouble for you. How long would you keep on coming back? Six months? A year? Two years?"

"So let's make a bargain on that, too. Six months. If you don't show up in six months, I'll know you aren't going to."

"You're a damned fool," said Frost. "I'm not going to contact you. I'm going to make a point not to. I don't want you involved. And, anyhow, six months is too long. In another month or so I'll have to start drifting south. I don't want to get caught up here by winter."

"Ann sent you a package," said Chapman, changing the subject to indicate that he would not yield on the contact business. "It's over there by the packing case. Needle and thread. Matches. Pair of scissors. A knife. Stuff like that she thought you might use. I guess there's some cans of food as well."

Frost nodded. "Tell Ann I'm thankful for the package. I'm grateful for what she tried to do. But tell her, for the love of God, to stand clear. Don't do any more. Don't try to do any more."

Chapman said, gravely, "I'll tell her."

"And thanks to you, too. You shouldn't have let her talk you into it."

"Once I knew about you," said Chapman, "she couldn't have talked me out of it. But answer me a question, if you will. How did it all happen? You told Ann you were in some sort of trouble. I figure someone framed you."

"Someone did," said Frost.

"You want to tell me more?"

"No, I don't. Ann and you probably would go digging into it, trying to prove it. And it can't be done. No one can. It's all down, legal, on the books."

"So you'll just sit here doing nothing?"

"Not entirely. Some day I'll figure out how to even up the score with Appleton . . ."

"Then it was Appleton?"

"Who else?" asked Frost. "And maybe you ought to get out of here. You make me talk too much. Stay around and I'll spill my guts and I don't want that."

Chapman got up slowly. "O.K.," he said, "I'll go. I hate to. Doesn't seem I have done too much."

He started to move away, then stopped and turned around.

"I have a gun," he said. "If you . . ."

Frost shook his head emphatically. "No," he said, fiercely. "What do you want me to do, cancel out the one right that I have? You'd better get rid of it. You know that they're illegal—any kind of gun."

"It doesn't bother me," said Chapman. "I'll keep it. I have even less to lose than you have."

He turned around and moved toward the door.

"Chapman," Frost said softly.

"Yes."

"Thanks for coming. It was good of you. I'm not quite myself."

"I understand," said Chapman.

Then he was through the door and pulling it shut behind him. Frost listened to him going up the stairs and out into the alley and finally the footfalls faded into silence.

23

WOULD the lilacs smell as sweet, Mona Campbell wondered, when spring came around a thousand years from now? Could one still catch the breath in wonder at the sight of a meadow filled with daffodils, a thousand years from now? If there were, a thousand years from now, any room on earth for lilac or for daffodil.

She sat, rocking gently back and forth, in the rocker she'd found up in the attic and had carried down the stairs to wipe the dust and cobwebs off it, looking out the window at the full-leafed wonder of a late June dusk. In a little while there would be lightning bugs and the first faint smell of fog from the river valley.

She sat and rocked and the soft benediction of the summer evening fell in all its fullness on her, and in all the world, for this moment, there was nothing more important than just sitting there, rocking back and forth, looking out the window at the green that turned to black as the shadows deepened and the cool of the night hours settled down to chase away all but the memory of the hot blast of the daytime sun.

But here, right now, whispered one small portion of her brain that fought to stay efficient, was the place and time to start forming the decision that she had to make.

But the whisper died in the silence and the deepening darkness. And the fantasy, although it was far from fantasy, crept in to take the place of the brain's efficiency.

A fantasy, she thought—of course it's fantasy, it must be fantasy. For in this place and time, in this dusk, in this smell of new and damp and reawakened earth, it could never be. For here the smell of vital earth, the flitting lantern of the firefly, the appointed fall of dusk and the appointed brightening of the dawn spoke of cycles, and life and death must also be an intrinsic part of such a cosmic cycling.

And this was the thought, she told herself, that she must remember through all the aeons that stretched ahead of mankind—not as a race, not as a species, but as individuals. But it was a thought, she knew, that she would not remember. For it was not a thought of youth. Rather, it was the thought of someone such as she—a middle-aged and dowdy woman who too long had been concerned with matters that were unwomanly. Mathematics—what had a woman to do with mathematics other than the basic arithmetic of fitting the family's budget to the family's need? And what had a woman to do with life other than the giving and the rearing of new life? And why must she, Mona Campbell, be compelled to reach a decision, all alone, that only God Himself (if, indeed, there were such an entity as God) should be called upon to make?

If she could only know what the world might be like a thousand years from now—not in its external aspects, for its external aspects would be no more than cultural coloration, but what it might be like in the core of mankind, in the hearts of men and women. What kind of world could there be, or would there be, when all of humankind lived eternally and in the flesh and guise of youth? Would wisdom come without gray hair and wrinkled brow? Would the old, long thoughts of aged people disappear and die in the exuberance of the flesh and gland and muscle that renewed itself? Would the gentleness and the tolerance and the long reflective thought no longer be with mankind? Would man ever again be able to sit in a rocking chair and gaze out an open window at the advent of the evening and find there, in that advancement of the darkness, an occasion for contentment?

Or might youth itself be no more than a trapping and a coloration? Would mankind finally sink into an atmosphere of futility, impatient with the endless days, disillusioned and disappointed with eternity? After the millionth mating, after the billionth piece of pumpkin pie, after a hundred thousand springs with lilac and with daffodil, what would there be left?

Did man need more than life?

Could he do with less than death?

And these were questions, she knew, that she could not answer, but they were questions to which, in fairness to herself, if not to all those others, answers must be found.

She rocked gently back and forth and let the questions and the nagging of them flow out of her, and slowly the soft wonder of the evening flowed in to erase them entirely from her thoughts.

Down in some unknown, darkened hollow folded in the hills the first of the whippoorwills began its evening chant.

24

Now that the beard had grown so heavy that it all but obscured the marks of ostracism on his cheek, Frost did not need to wait for dark, but could venture out when dusk began to fall. With an old battered hat he had retrieved from a trash bin pulled down almost to his eyes, he began his prowling as soon as the streets began to clear of the surging mobs which poured through them in the daylight hours. At dusk the city was left to him. Only a few people then remained upon the streets and they went scurrying past him, on urgent erands of their own, as if there might be some high reason that they not stay out of doors, but must hurry to get back to their huddling places, somewhere within the interminable warrens of the great apartment houses which rose like ancient monuments reared by brutelike monsters in the primeval past.

Frost, observing them from beneath the brim of his pulled-down hat, knew how it was with them, for once it had been the same with him. Hurry and huddle—hurry so that one could gather all the assets he could manage, then huddle in his idle time so that he would not spend a single penny of those assets.

Although now, even had they wished to spend some of the assets on rather foolish things, there was no longer any way to do it. For there were no longer any movies, no longer any athletic contests, and the fabled night life of a century and a half ago had died in the stagnation of the urge to live forever. All of which, of course, pleased Forever Center (if Forever Center, in fact, had not planned it that way) for it meant that there was more money to be invested in Forever stock.

So with the end of the day's activity, the human herd went home and there, for entertainment, read the daily papers, which had ceased long since to be informational, but were frankly and entertainingly sensational. Or read cheap books, cheap in price and often cheap in content. Or sat slack-jawed and fascinated before the family TV set. Or, perhaps, gloated over a stamp collection which had appreciated in value steadily through the years, or perhaps a collection of chess sets, wonderfully carved or fabricated, or many other similar collections in which each owner had carefully (and prayerfully) risked some of his surplus assets.

And there were those, as well, who resorted to hallucinatory drugs, available at any drug counter, using them to give themselves a few hours of an imaginary life—a life in which they could escape from the drabness and the monotony of their regular lives.

For now there was nothing new, as there had been in ages past. Once, back at the beginning of the twentieth century, there had been the phonograph to be excited over . . . and the telephone. And later there had been the airplane and the radio and later yet, TV. But today there was nothing new. There was no progress except in those areas which advanced the day toward which Forever Center pointed. Now man made do with what he had and in most cases what he had was less than his forebears had. Civilization had ground to a stagnating halt and the life of man today was in many of its aspects the same cultural pattern as had been the pattern of the Dark Ages of more than a thousand years before.

In those days the peasants had worked the fields in daylight, performing their labors for no more than enough to keep themselves alive, and then had spent the night huddled in their hovels, with doors tight barred against the terrors of the dark.

And it was the same today—hurry through the day, huddle through the night. Hurry and huddle—waiting out the night to hurry once again.

But for Frost there was now no need to hurry. To skulk, perhaps, but never need to hurry. For there were few places he had to go and none of them held great urgency. He went each evening to pick up the package left for him beside the garbage can; he hunted through occasional trash containers for papers to serve his daytime reading, keeping his eyes open for any other discarded items which might be of interest to him. He read and slept through the daylight hours and at dusk again began his prowling.

There were others like himself, prowlers of the darkened and deserted streets, and at times he spoke briefly with them, for he could not harm such as these, he told himself, by talking with them. And once, in a vacant area on the waterfront, where an old building had been newly razed, he had sat around a fire with two other men and had talked with them, but when he went back the next night they were gone and there was no fire. He formed no associations with these other prowlers of the dark, nor did any of them try to prolong an acquaintance with him. Loners, all of them— and at times he wondered who they might be and who they might have been and why they walked the night. But he knew he could not ask and they never told him and this was not strange, for he did not identify himself.

Perhaps it was because he no longer had an identity. No longer Daniel Frost, but a human zero. No better off, of no more consequence than any of those millions who slept in the streets of India, who had rags to cover them and, sometimes, not even rags, who had never known any other state than hunger, who long since had given up even the right or the wish to find a private place in which to go about the private functions of the body.

For a time Frost had expected that one of the Holies would seek him out again, but this did not happen. Although he saw, in his prowling, evidence that they were still about and active—slogans hurriedly chalked upon the vacant walls:

FRIEND, DON'T FALL FOR IT!
WHY SETTLE FOR LESS THAN REAL IMMORTALITY?
WHAT ABOUT GREAT-GRANDPA?
OUR FOREBEARS WEREN'T DOPES—BUT WE ARE DUPES.

and again and again and again, the new one:

WHY CALL THEM BACK FROM HEAVEN?

With the practiced eye of a professional sloganeer, Frost admired the work. Better in many ways, he thought, than the smug, conservative junk that he and his department had figured out and which still flashed off and on in luridly lit letters high atop many of the buildings, the official watchwords of Forever Center—many of them frankly stolen from a day much earlier:

WASTE NOT, WANT NOT.
A PENNY SAVED IS A PENNY EARNED.

Even the new ones sweated out in all earnestness

DON'T KID YOURSELF—YOU'LL NEED IT!
NOW YOU CAN TAKE IT WITH YOU!
STICK WITH FOREVER; FOREVER STICKS WITH YOU.

seemed rather pallid now that he could view them from an observer's viewpoint.

So he prowled the streets alone, without a purpose, with no destination. Not running any longer. Restless at first, but now no longer restless; no longer the nervous pacing of a caged feline, but now the strolling of a man who, for the first time in his life, through no choice of his own, but through shame and outrage, had become something of what it seemed to him a man had ought to be. A man who, for the first time, saw the stars through the city's haze and speculated upon the wonder and the distance of them, who listened to the talking of the river as it went rolling down the land, who took the time to appreciate the architecture of a tree.

Not always like this, of course, but many times like this. At other times the rage and the anger and the shame took hold of him and smoldered like a bonfire in his guts, and at times, cold with the selfsame rage and shame, he worked out elaborate and fantastic, and utterly illogical, campaigns for vengeance—never plans for his rehabilitation, for his return to the normal world of men, but always plans for vengeance.

He lived and slept and walked and ate what the man at the restaurant left for him by the garbage cans—a half a loaf of stale bread, the trimmings from a roast, a roll, a dried-out piece of pie, and many other things. Now at times he stood in the alley, waiting, not bothering to hide, until the man put the bundle out, then raised his arm in greeting and in gratitude, and the man would wave back at him. No word and no approach, never more than this wave of greeting, this semaphoring of a common brotherhood, but it seemed to Frost that the man still was known to him and that he was a long-time friend.

Once Frost started on a pilgrimage, heading back toward the neighborhood where he once had lived, but still blocks away from it he had turned around and returned to the alley where he now resided. For halfway there, he had realized that there was nothing for him to go back to, that he had left there nothing of himself. In the entry hall his name now would be replaced upon the board by another name, and another car, exactly like his car (for all cars were alike), would be parked with a row of identical cars, their noses pressed against the blank brick wall back of the apartment house. But his car would be gone, hauled away long days before under confiscatory order. And the building itself meant no more to him than the ramshackle building, the basement of which he occupied. For now the basement was his home. In this age, he knew, any hole was home.

Back in his basement he sat in the dark and tried once again to think his situation through, trying to marshal the factors into neat progression, hoping to find in all those straightly aligned facets of the position in which he found himself some road along which he most logically should move. But it was a road he had not found as yet and the picket fence of facts spelled nothing but a dead end.

It was no better this time. He was trapped and there was no road but one, that last, desperate, bitter road into the vaults where his body would be stored. That road he would not take until he was forced to take it. For, as things stood now, if he went into the vaults, he would come out of them a pauper, no better equipped to deal with his second life than the tribesman in Central Africa, no better than the peon from South America, on the selfsame basis as the man who slept in the streets of India. If he stayed alive, perhaps somewhere, somehow—when or how he could not guess—he might stumble onto some opportunity or some situation which might yield a competence, perhaps a very modest one, but at least something upon which he could start his second life.

Perhaps he would not be able to live the kind of life the really wealthy ones would live, would not belong among the billionaires. But at least he would not stand in bread lines or shiver in the street for the lack of shelter. In the kind of world one would waken into, it would be better to be dead than poor.

He shuddered as he thought of what it would be like to be poor in that glittering world of wealth, in that world where men would wake and find their savings many times increased. And wealth such as this would be solid wealth, for it would represent the very earth itself. By the time that the stockholders of Forever Center came back to second life every facility and every material thing upon the entire planet would be represented in that stock. The men who held the stock, with prudence of any kind at all, would go on being rich. And the man who held none of the stock would never have a chance; he would be condemned to remain a pauper through all eternity.

Thinking of it, he knew that for that reason, if no other, he could never think of going to the vaults.

And he would not go to the vaults for another reason. It was the thing that Marcus Appleton had expected him to do.

Looking down the avenue of time, he saw the endless days stretching interminably ahead, like so many trees that lined the avenue. But there was no other road, no other way that he could go other than this blind and endless avenue leading on to nowhere.

He slept away the day and in the evening set out on his prowling once again.

Night had fallen when he walked into the alley to pick up the package beside the garbage can. The package was not there and he knew from this that he had arrived too early. The man had not come out yet.

He retired to the dark angle of a wall that jutted out farther in the alley than the next adjoining wall and hunkered down to wait.

A cat came padding softly in the shadow, alert and anxious. It halted and stared at Frost, crouching in his angle. Apparently deciding that he was no danger to it, the cat sat down and began to wash its face.

Then the back door of the restaurant opened and a shaft of light speared out into the night. The man came out, his white coat shining in the light, a basket of garbage resting on his right hip and clutched by his right hand, a package in his left.

Frost rose and took a step out toward the alley. A flat report smote against the lane of walls and the man in white straightened in a spasm, his head thrown back, his body tensed and straining. The basket dropped and spun slowly on its bottom rim, spilling the dark litter of the garbage.

Frost caught one glimpse of the man's face, in the second before the body crumpled—a white blur with a spreading darkness on it, running from the hairline.

The white-coated man was down, huddled on the pavement, and the basket, still spinning, came to a stop when it rolled against his body.

Frost took another step out toward the alley, then stopped, poised and tensed.

The cat was gone. Nothing stirred. There was no shout, no footstep.

Frost's brain screamed at him: *A trap!*

A man dead in the alley, gunned down, more than likely with brain damage (darkness sluicing down his face) that would rule out any possibility of a second life.

A man dead in the alley and he waiting in the alley, and, Frost was very sure, a gun that could be found.

This was death for him, he knew. No longer ostracism, but final death—not normal death, but the terminal cancellation that did away with life. For a man who would kill, in cold blood, a man who had befriended him could expect nothing else but death.

And it would make no difference that he hadn't killed the man—no more difference than it had made that he'd not committed treason.

He spun around and stared at the walls.

Both of them were brick, the buildings two stories high, thirty feet or so. But on the one that was farther back from the alley apparently there once had been a shed extending out over the back door. The shed was no longer there, but jutting out from the smooth brick wall was a series of half-bricks, an inverted V, which had at one time formed the support for the roof timbers of the shed.

Frost took three running strides and leaped. His fingers caught and hooked over the lower extending brick and for a breathless micro-second he feared that the brick might break or slide out of its place from the pressure of his weight. But it held and he reached quickly up with his left hand and caught the second brick and hauled himself up, with his right hand closing on the third brick, so his left could reach the fourth.

Driven by a desperate panic, he swarmed up the wall, hand over hand, his muscles powered by a strength he did not know he had, his nerves a hardened knot of urgency.

As he reached the fifth brick up, he got a foot on the lower brick and hurled himself upward in a mighty surge. His elbows caught the top of the wall and he hauled himself swiftly over it and fell flat upon the roof. A two-foot upward projection of the wall hid him from the alley.

He lay there, panting with the exertion of his climb, pressed against the asphalt of the roof, and out in the alley he heard the rapidly running footsteps and the harsh shouts of horror.

He could not stay here, he knew. He must somehow get away, not only from the roof and alley, but from his neighborhood. When they did not find him in the alley, they then would search the rooftops and the buildings on each side of the alley and by that time he must be many blocks away.

He turned his head on one side and looked across the roof. A small projection above the level rooftop caught his eyes and he crawled toward it.

Down in the alley the shouting was louder now and added to it was the distant howling of the rescue wagon's siren. Right on time, thought Frost, but little good it would do the man lying in the alley. The bullet must have caught him squarely in the brain.

He reached the projection and saw that it was a square cap, made of wood and covered by metal, apparently covering a hatch.

His fingers worked at the edge of it, seeking for a hold, but the cap was fitted tight. With a hand on each side of it, he twisted and it seemed to give. He twisted again and it seemed to lift. He put more power into the twist and suddenly the cap was free and lifting. And even as he lifted it, he wondered what he would find on that floor below.

Slowly he tilted the cap up and the area under it was

dark. He breathed a little easier, although he knew that he was not entirely in the clear. There might be someone down there. It could be merely the top floor of a store or it could be living quarters.

He lifted the cap entirely off and set it to one side, then lowered himself into the hatch. He hung by his arms for a moment, his body extended. The place was dark, although a little light seemed to come from somewhere. Reason said there must be a floor beneath him, but he felt, as he hung there, that he was poised above a pit.

He let loose and dropped. He fell two feet or so. Something that he bumped into went over with a crash. The wind half knocked out of him, Frost crouched on the floor, ears strained for any sound.

Outside, the siren of the rescue wagon ground to a shuddering silence. Someone, bull-throated, was shouting, but the muffled words were lost. Within the room itself there was no sound at all.

Darker shapes became evident as his eyes became accustomed to the gloom. Faint light seeped into the area, which he now saw was no partitioned room, but the entire space of the second floor, from the tall, narrow windows that fronted on the street.

He saw the shapes were furniture, crouching chairs, embattled chests, squat tables. The display floor of a small and dingy furniture establishment.

He should replace the cap, he thought, for searchers, finding it, would guess where he had gone. But it might be hard to do and would take more time than he could afford. He'd have to find something to stand on to reach the hatch, would have to wrestle the cap into position, with the good possibility that it would fail, despite all that he could do, to fall into full position.

He couldn't take the time, he told himself. He must be out of here before the hunt shifted from the alley to spread, perhaps, to the street outside.

He stumbled about the area, finally found the stairs, and went down them to the lower floor.

Here the light filtering through the display windows in the front was stronger than it had been upstairs.

At the door he turned back the knob of the night lock, released the regular latch, and pulled the door partway open, staring through the grimy glass at the street outside. The street seemed to be empty.

He opened the door and slid outside, pulling it to, but not latching it. He might need to get back through that door and thus under cover very quickly. Squeezing tight against the front of the building, he glanced quickly up and down the street.

There was no one.

Sprinting, he crossed the street, reached the corner, went around it, slowed to a rapid walk. Two blocks away he met another walker, but the man went past with barely a glance. There were a few cars and he slid into shadowed doorways until they'd gone past.

Half an hour later he began to feel he'd made it, that for the moment he was safe.

Safe, but running once again.

He could not, he knew, go back to the basement. For Appleton and his men would know about that hideout, must have watched him while they fabricated their conspiracy against him, the masterstroke that was intended to erase forever whatever threat he might represent to Appleton and Lane.

And what was that threat? he wondered. What did the paper mean? And had the paper actually been among the papers he'd put in the envelope for Ann?

Thinking about the envelope and Ann, he felt a pang of panic. If Appleton knew she had that paper, or suspected that she had it, she was in deadly danger. As everyone whose life touched his seemed in deadly danger. The man at the restaurant had done no more than a compassionate act for an unknown fellowman and now, because of this, lay dead, shot down with no other thought than how his death might contribute to the entrapment and the death of the man he had befriended.

Appleton must know that Ann had talked with him. More than likely it had been her appearance on the scene (signaling the belief that he was about to make some move?) which had triggered his seizure and his condemnation.

Perhaps, he thought, he should somehow warn her. But how was he to warn her? A phone call, but he had no money for a call. And a phone call, in any case, would be a stupid move, for in all probability her phone would be tapped. And she, herself, watched.

Or contact Chapman? But that, as well, was dangerous—not only to himself but to Chapman and to Ann. For it was likely that Appleton knew Chapman had come to see him and it would need no great imagination to connect Chapman with Ann.

The best thing he could do, Frost told himself, was to stay away from both of them. They should be warned, both of them, but in the warning he'd likely do more harm than if they never knew.

He settled down to a steady, dogged trudging, keeping to the shadows as much as possible. It was essential, he knew, to put as much distance between himself and the alley where the man had died as he could. But well before dawn he must find a place to hide, a den where he could crouch through the daylight hours. And when night came he must push on again to build an even greater distance between himself and the wrath that trailed him.

25

Two old men met in a park for a game of checkers.

"You hear the latest," asked one old codger, "about this Forever business?"

"You hear so much," said the other one, setting up the pieces, "that you hardly know what story to believe. They say now that if they get this immortality business worked out, you won't have to die at all. They'll just line everybody up, every blessed one of us, and jab us in the arm and then we'll get young again and we'll live forever. Won't that be something, now?"

The old codger shook his head. "That ain't what I had in mind. Got this direct. My nephew has a brother-in-law who works in one of them Forever labs and it was him that told it. I can tell you there are a lot of people who'll be in for a big surprise."

"What surprise?" the second asked, impatiently.

"Well, maybe that's not the word exactly. Maybe they won't be surprised. Hard to be surprised, I suppose, when you go on being dead."

"You're rambling on again," complained his partner. "Why can't you ever come right out and say what is on your mind?"

"I was just laying the foundation. Giving you the background."

"Well, get on with it so we can start this game."

"It seems," the old codger told him, "that they've found there is some sort of bacteria—I think that's what he said—some sort of bacteria that lives inside the brain and that this bacteria can go right on living when the body's frozen. The brain is frozen solid, but this bacteria isn't bothered whatsoever. It goes right on living, multiplying all the time, and eating at the brain."

121

"I don't believe it," said the other. "You hear such stories all the time and I tell you, John, there ain't a lick of truth in any one of them. I wouldn't be surprised if them Holies don't start them stories just to befuddle us. If we got this bacteria in the brain, how come it don't eat up the brain while we are still alive?"

"Well, that's just it," said John. "When we are alive, there's something in the brain—antibodies, would they be? —that hold them bacteria in check. But when the brain is frozen it can't make them antibodies and the bacteria run wild. I tell you, there are a lot of people in those vaults who have no brain at all, just an empty skull crammed full of bacteria."

26

FROST came to a decision; to carry out the decision, he stole an automobile.

The theft was not an easy task. He had to find a car in which the forgetful owner had left the key. He knew, vaguely, that there was a way by which one could juggle ignition wires to start the motor without a key, but he had no idea how to go about it. Besides, he had an unreasonable fear of electricity and, thus, a disinclination to fool around with wires.

On the fourth night of his search, he found a car parked behind a food market with the key in the ignition. He scouted the area to make sure that no one was around to raise an alarm when he took the car. More than likely, he reasoned, it belonged to someone working late in the market. There were lighted windows in the back of the place, but they were located too high for him to reach them in an attempt to see who might be there.

He slid beneath the wheel and started the motor. Holding his breath, he eased the machine out of the parking area and down the ramp to the street. It was not until he was a dozen blocks away that he resumed his normal breathing.

Half an hour later he stopped the car and rummaged in the tool kit, coming up with a small screwdriver. A mile or so farther on, in a residential area where the street was dark because of the great elms which lined the boulevard, he parked behind another car. Working without light and by feel, and as quietly as he could, he switched the license plates of the car he'd stolen with the one parked in the street.

Driving off, he told himself it might have been a waste of time to make the switch of plates, but within a few hours someone would report a stolen car and the switching of the plates might give him a slightly better chance to go on undetected.

There was little traffic, here on the west edge of the city. Night after night, as he had hunted for a car that he could steal, he had worked his way westward, heading for the city's edge and the wilderness beyond. There, even from the first night of his flight from the alley, he had reasoned he'd have a better chance to hide. Such population as there might be was scattered and there were great areas which had reverted back from farmland to heavy second growth. And also, in the back of his mind, was a persistent feeling that Appleton would not suspect that he would leave the city.

There would be problems, he knew, away from the city. Food, for one thing. But he had a vague confidence, not too well founded, that he could manage. The season for fruit and berries was approaching and he could catch some fish and perhaps devise traps for the snaring of small animals. Thanks to Ann, he was at least partially equipped. Stowed in his pockets, put there in the knowledge that at any moment he might have to leave his basement den, were the small items which she had sent him—fishhooks and line, a pocket lighter with a can of fluid and extra flints and wicks, a heavy pocketknife, a small pair of shears, a comb, a can opener (for which he would have no use, certainly, in the wilderness), and a small medical kit. With these, he was sure that he could manage, although he did not know exactly how.

He did not allow any of his half-recognized problems worry him too much. All his resources now were directed at leaving the city behind—to find a place where he would not be forever dodging or crouching, always fearful that he would be sighted by some citizen and reported as a suspicious character.

The idea of fleeing to the wilderness had formed in his mind on the first night of his flight. It was not until later that he had decided he would head further west than he had at first intended—back to the old farm where he had spent vacations in his youth. He had fought against the decision, for the surface of his mind protested it was a silly thing to do, but even as the surface of his mind protested, some more powerful inner mind drove him on finally to decide against what seemed his better judgment.

In the daytime, as he huddled in his hiding places, he had tried to unravel the reasons for the urge that drove him to seek this place out of his youth. Was it, perhaps, a need to identify himself with something? Was it the unrecognized, but crying need to stand on familiar ground, to say this is a place that I know and that knows me and we belong to one another—a seeking after roots, no matter how shallow they might be?

He did not know. He could not know. He was only aware that something more powerful than his own good common sense impelled him toward this old and abandoned farm.

And now, finally, he was on his way.

He could have made better time by using one of the great freeways that leaped in all directions from the city. But these he avoided, these he could not force himself to take. He had hidden and crouched too long to expose himself to the traffic he would encounter there.

He had no map and no sure notion of where he might be going. The one thing that he knew was that he was heading west. The moon had been sliding down the western sky when he had found the car and now he followed the moon.

For an hour or more he had been driving through residential areas, interspersed with small shopping centers. Now he began to encounter large open spaces which lay between little settlements. He found a road, not a street, but a road, narrow and ill-paved, and he followed it.

The road dwindled to little more than a track and the paving ended and the track was coated with a deep and heavy dust. The houses became fewer, then almost none at all. Great clumps of woods loomed black against the sky.

At the top of a long, bald ridge which the road climbed with many twistings and turnings, he finally stopped the car and got out, turning to look back.

Behind him, stretching east and north and south, as far as the eye could see, were the lights of the city he had left. Ahead of him was darkness with no single gleam of light.

He stood atop the ridge and drew great gulping breaths of air into his lungs—air that had about it the freshness and the chilliness of the open land. And there was, as well, the smell of pine and dust—and he had finally made it. The city was behind him.

He got back in the car and drove on. The road got no

better and he could make no good time on it, but it was still a road and it bored straight into the west.

At dawn he pulled off it, bumped across a shallow roadside ditch, drove through an old field overgrown with weeds and brush, and parked in a grove of oaks at one end of the field.

He got out of the car and stretched and his gut was gaunt with hunger, but this morning, he told himself, for the first time in weeks, he'd not have to hunt a hole to hide in.

27

After waiting for an hour, Ann Harrison got in to see Marcus Appleton.

The man was affable. Behind his desk he had the look of a prosperous, efficient businessman.

"Miss Harrison," he said, "I am so glad to see you. I've read so much about you. In connection, I believe, with a certain point you raised in a trial of some sort."

"Not that it did my client any good," said Ann.

"But still it was well worth raising. It's from thinking such as this that the law evolves."

"I thank you for the compliment," said Ann. "If it was a compliment."

"Oh, yes," said Appleton. "I was most sincere. And now, I wonder, would you tell me to what I owe this meeting? What can I do for you?"

"For one thing," said Ann, "you can remove the taps you have upon my phones. For another, you can call off the bloodhounds you have set to follow me. And you can tell me what it's all about."

"But my dear young lady . . ."

"You can save your breath," Ann told him. "I know you have the taps. Perhaps at the central switchboard. I have prepared actions against both you and the communications people which will enjoin you from an invasion of my privacy and the privacy of my clients, which might be much more to the point than my own privacy and . . ."

"You can't get away with it," Appleton said, harshly.

"I think I can," said Ann. "No court would ignore such a situation. It strikes directly at the guarantees which are accorded the relationship of an attorney and the client. And it strikes as well at the roots of justice."

"You have no proof."

"I think I have," said Ann. "That is not a matter I'll discuss with you. But even if my proof were not quite sufficient, and I believe it is, I still imagine that the court would order an inquiry into the charges that I brought."

"That's preposterous!" exploded Appleton. "The courts haven't got the time, or the purpose, to inquire into every piddling charge someone may bring before them."

"Perhaps not every charge. But a charge of this kind . . ."

"You'll probably end up," Appleton told her, coldly, "getting yourself disbarred."

"Perhaps," said Ann. "If you own the courts as thoroughly as you think you own them. I don't think you own them that much."

Appleton sputtered. "Own the courts!" he yelled.

"Why, yes," Ann said, calmly. "The courts and the newspapers. But you don't own the rumors. They're something that you don't control. And if the courts should try to shush me and if the papers remained silent, there still would be a stink. Believe me, Mr. Appleton, I'd see there was a stink such as you've never smelled before."

The sputter died. "You're threatening me?" he asked in a cold voice so sharp it almost squeaked.

"Oh, I don't suppose," said Ann, "it would ever come to that. I still have faith in justice as dispensed by law. I still believe the courts hold forth some hope of remedy. And I'm not too sure you have all the papers muzzled."

"You have no high opinion of Forever Center?"

"Why should I have?" she asked. "You've gobbled everything. You've suppressed everything. You've held off progress. You've turned the people into clods. There still are governments, but they are shadow governments that jump at your slightest hint. And against all this you plead that you offer something, and you do offer something, but do you have to place so high a price on it?"

"All right," he said. "If your phones are tapped and we removed the taps and if we called off what you call our bloodhounds, what more would you want?"

"You won't, of course," said Ann, "do any of these things. But if you did, there'd still be one further thing you could do for me. You could tell me why."

"Miss Harrison," said Appleton, "I'll be as frank with you as you have been with me. If we've paid you any undue attention it's because we're very curious concerning your relationship with Daniel Frost."

"I have no relationship with him. I saw him only once."

"You did go to visit him?"

"I went to ask his help for a client of mine."

"For this Franklin Chapman?"

"When you talk of Franklin Chapman, I wish you'd change your tone of voice. The man was convicted under an obsolete and vicious law that is a part of this terrible reign of frantic desperation Forever Center has imposed upon the world."

"You asked Frost's help for Chapman?"

She nodded. "He told me there was nothing he could do, but that if ever, in the future, there was some way to help my client he would do it."

"Then Frost is not your client."

"He is not," she said.

"He gave you a paper."

"He gave me an envelope. It was sealed. I don't know if anything was in it."

"And he still is not your client?"

"Mr. Appleton, as one human being, he entrusted me, another human being, with an envelope. That is quite a simple matter. It need not become involved in legal complications."

"Where is that envelope?"

"Why," said Ann, in some surprise, "I thought perhaps you had it. Some of your men went through my office very thoroughly. Also my apartment. I had thought, of course, you'd found it. If you haven't got it, I can't imagine where it is."

Appleton sat quietly behind his desk, staring at her, so still that even his eyelids didn't move.

"Miss Harrison," he finally said, "you are the coolest customer I have ever met."

"I walk into lions' dens," said Ann. "I'm not afraid of lions."

Appleton idly flipped a hand. "You and I," he said, "talk a common language. You came to make a deal."

"I came," she said, "to get you off my neck."

"The envelope," he said, "and Frost is reinstated."

"His sentence reversed," she said, bitterly. "The tattoos

removed. His estate and job restored. His memories wiped away and the rumors stilled."

He nodded. "We could talk about it."

"Why, how wonderful of you," she said. "When you could kill him just as easily."

"Miss Harrison," he said sadly, "you must think that we are monsters."

"Of course I do," she said.

"The envelope?" he asked.

"I imagine that you have it."

"And if we don't?"

"Then I don't know where it is. And all of this is pointless, anyhow. I didn't come here to make what you call a deal."

"But since you're here?"

She shook her head. "I have no authority. Any talk of this sort must be with Daniel Frost."

"You could tell him."

"Yes," she said, lightly, "I suppose I could."

Appleton leaned forward just a bit too quickly, like a man who tried to show no eagerness at all, but was trapped into showing it.

"Then perhaps you should," he said.

"I was about to add that I could mention it to him if I knew where he was. Really, Mr. Appleton, there is so little point to this. I have no interest in it and I doubt that Mr. Frost would have a great deal more."

"But Frost . . ."

"He'd know as well as I," said Ann, "that he couldn't trust you."

She rose from the chair and walked toward the door. Appleton came awkwardly to his feet and stepped around the desk.

"On this other matter," he said.

"I've decided," Ann told him, "that I should file my petitions. It just occurs to me I shouldn't trust you, either."

Going down the elevator, she had her first moments of deep doubt. What, she asked herself, had she actually accomplished? Well, for one thing, she had placed him on notice that she knew she was being watched. And she had learned, of course, that he knew no more than she did where Daniel Frost might be.

She went across the foyer and out into the parking lot and there, beside her car, stood a tall, bony, grizzled man. His hair was gray and his whiskers—not a beard, but simply unshaved whiskers—were salt and pepper shade.

When he saw her approaching, he opened the door and said, "Miss Harrison, you don't know me, but I am a friend and you need a friend. You have been up to talk with Appleton and . . ."

"Please," said Ann. "Please leave me alone."

"I'm George Sutton," he told her, quietly, "and I'm a Holy. Appleton would give a lot to get his hands on me. I was born a Holy and I'll always be one. If you don't believe me, look."

He tore his shirtfront open and pointed to the right side of the chest.

"No incision scar," he said. "There's no transmitter in me."

"The scar could have disappeared."

"You're wrong," he said. "It always leaves a scar. As you grow up, new transmitters must be implanted. You get your final transmitter when you're well into your teens."

"Get in the car," she told him, sharply. "If you don't, someone will notice us. And if you're not a Holy . . ."

"You think, perhaps, that I'm a man from Forever Center. You think . . ."

"Get in the car," she said.

Out in the street the car was swallowed by the great flowing traffic river.

"I saw Daniel Frost," said Sutton, "that first night. One of my men brought him to our hideout and I talked with him . . ."

"What did you say to him?"

"Many things. We talked about our slogan campaign and he thought poorly of it. And I asked him if he read the Bible and if he believed in God. I always ask that of people. Miss, that was a funny question that you asked—what we talked about. What difference does it make?"

"Because I know something of what you talked about."

"You have seen him, then?"

"No. I haven't seen him."

"There was another man . . ."

"It was the other man," she said. "Dan told him you had asked about the Bible and if he believed in God."

"So now you're satisfied about me."

"I don't know," she said, her voice tense and tight. "I suppose I am, although I can't be sure. It all has been a nightmare. Not knowing anything. Being watched. I knew they were watching me; I saw them. And I am positive that my phone was tapped. I couldn't just sit still. I couldn't simply sit and take it. That's why I went to Appleton. And you—you've been watching, too!"

He nodded. "You and Frost and this other man—this Chapman. Miss, we don't merely paint the slogans on the walls. We do many other things. We fight Forever Center in every way we can."

"But why?"

"Because they are our enemies; they're the enemies of mankind. We're all that's left of the old mankind. We are the underground. We've been driven underground."

"I don't mean that. I mean why are you watching us?"

"I suppose that's part of it. But we can help you, too. We were standing by the night the man was killed, behind the restaurant. We were ready to be of help, but Frost didn't need our help."

"And you know where he is?"

"No. We know he stole a car. We figure that he left the city. We lost him, but the last we saw of him he was heading west."

"And you thought that I might know."

"Well, no, we didn't think so. We'd not have contacted you if you'd not gone to Forever Center."

"What has that to do with it? I had the right . . ."

"You had the right, of course. But now Appleton knows that you know he is watching you. So long as you played stupid and said nothing, you were safe."

"Now I suppose I'm no longer safe."

"You can't fight Forever Center," he told her. "No one person can. There'll be an accident, something will happen. We have seen it happen in other instances."

"But I have something that he wants."

"Not something that he wants. Something, rather, that he wants no one else to have. The answer is quite simple. With

Frost out of the way and you out of the way, he'll be in the clear."

"You know all about this?"

"Miss," said Sutton, "I'd be downright simple if I didn't have my pipelines into Forever Center."

And this was it, she thought. No ordinary band of religious fanatics, no simple slogan painters, but a well-organized and efficient band of rebels who through the years, working quietly, and no doubt with daring, had caused Forever Center more trouble than anyone realized.

But doomed to failure. For no one could stand against the force and strength of a structure that, in effect, was owner of the world and that, furthermore, held out the promise of eternal life.

Into a structure such as this, there surely would be pipelines. Not only by the Holies but by anyone who might stand to gain. And with the greed occasioned by the driving need to establish an estate against the second life, there always would be those who would provide the pipelines.

"I suppose that I should thank you," said Ann.

"No thanks are necessary."

"Where can I drop you?"

"Miss Harrison," Sutton said, "I have more to say to you and I hope you'll listen to me."

"Why, of course, I'll listen."

"This paper that you have . . ."

"So you want it, too."

"If something should happen to you, if . . ."

"No," said Ann. "It isn't mine. It belongs to Daniel Frost."

"But if it should be lost. It's a weapon, don't you see? I don't know what is in it, but we . . ."

"I know. You'd use anything that you could get. Anything at all. No matter how you got it. No matter what it was."

"You're not very complimentary, but I suppose that is the case."

"Mr. Sutton," Ann said, "I'm going to pull over to the curb. I'll slow up, but I won't stop. And I want you to get out."

"If you wish, miss."

133

"I do wish," she said. "And leave me alone. One is enough, trailing me and spying. I don't need two of you."

It had been a mistake going to see Marcus Appleton, she told herself. No matter what she might have thought or said, this was not something that could be resolved in a court of law. And a bluff, no matter how well managed, was no good at all. There was, it seemed, too much at stake and too many people who had an interest in what was going on. You could not dodge them all.

There was just one answer for this moment. She could not go back, not to her office, nor to her apartment. For now the squeeze was on and if she had her way about it, she would not be caught.

She slowed the car and Sutton stepped heavily to the curb.

"Thanks for the ride," he said.

"Don't mention it," she told him, and gunned the car back into the flowing traffic.

She had some money in her bag and her credit cards and there was no reason why she should go back.

On the lam, she thought. But not really on the lam. Going to someone, not running from someone.

God grant, she thought, that he's still all right!

28

He had swung far south of Chicago. Once, from far off, he had seen the distance-misted towers and blocks of masonry that rose beside the lower end of the lake. Now he was west of it and heading north, still following the tiny, twisting, old-time roads. At times they dwindled out or became impassable and he would be forced to turn around and retrace his way, looking for another of the primitive, grass-grown highways that trended in the right direction.

It had been like that all the way from the East Coast and he had not made good progress. Although there was no reason now that he should make good progress. There was no reason, he told himself time and time again, that he go anywhere. He had no actual destination; the destination that he did have was an emotion-charged fantasy in which there could be no real meaning and no purpose. The comfort and identity which it seemed to hold was no more than delusion; when he arrived it would be as empty and as barren as any mile along the road he took to reach it. But knowing this, he still made his way toward it, driven by an inner urge which he failed to understand.

He met few people. Through the areas he traveled there were few inhabitants. Occasionally there would be a down-at-heels family living—camping might be a better word—at one of the many abandoned sets of farm buildings. Occasionally there were tiny villages still inhabited, a few families still living there in a stubborn refusal to join the now all but completed movement to the vast urban centers, existing in a small nucleus of humanity surrounded by the empty and decaying structures which at one time had housed a healthy community.

At times he drove past monitor-and-rescue stations, with the rescue cars and helicopters standing on the ramp, ready at an instant to dash out to retrieve a body when the monitor housed within the building detected the cessation of a transmitter signal, indicating that a heart had stopped its beating, pegging with exactitude the geographic coordinates where the stoppage had occurred.

There could not, Frost imagined, be much work to do at stations such as these, for due to the thinly scattered population months might go by without a single death within the quadrant covered by a station. And yet, even in those areas where, for long periods of time, there might be no signal except for some transient passing through, the stations still were maintained against the chance that within the area some life might flicker out.

For, despite what might be said of it, despite the rumors and the watchful critics, Forever Center still kept the ancient faith, still carried on the tradition of service which was implicit in the purpose for which it had been founded. And that, Frost told himself, with a surge of pride, was the way it had to be. For faith was the one solid foundation upon which such a social structure could be built.

The roads he traveled did not allow the piling up of any great amount of mileage in any single day. The necessity of finding food delayed the progress further. He foraged for berries and from scraggy trees still surviving in old orchards he gathered early-ripened fruit. He fished with fair success in many tiny streams, in some larger rivers. From a strong hickory sapling he fashioned a bow and trimmed arrows from ash sprouts, spent hours in trying to learn how to handle the weapon he'd devised. But the bow and arrows did not pay for the time expended in the making of them. The only game he gathered with it was an ancient woodchuck, tough and stringy, but at least red meat, the first that he had tasted in many weeks.

In an abandoned farmhouse he found a kettle, with some rusty spots, but still intact. A few days later, on the edge of a scummy pond, he captured a snapping turtle that had strayed too far from water, butchered it, and put it in the kettle to boil. He was not entirely sure that he liked the soup, but it was food and that was the thing that counted.

He began to have a sense of leisure. No longer hiding, no longer running, he moved down a long and twisting avenue of contented time. Finding a camping place that appealed to him, he'd stay for several days, resting, fishing, swimming, foraging, and eating. He attempted to smoke some of the fish he caught, to build up a food supply against a future day. The experiment did not work out.

He no longer watched the road behind him. Marcus Appleton undoubtedly still was hunting for him, but the chances were, he told himself, that he had not learned as yet his prey had left the city. The theft of the car would have been long since reported, the car to which he'd switched the plates might have been discovered, but there was no way, he felt sure, that the theft could be traced to him. The recognition and recovery of a stolen car was not an easy thing, for all cars were alike, all turned out by one company, which no longer bothered, since there was no competition and no customer demand, to change the models every year—or every ten or twenty years.

For the cars were standard, engineered to certain well-established specifications. All small, so they took less space. All powered by long-life batteries—silent, fumeless, slow of speed, all with low centers of gravity. The kind of car to fit the crowded street conditions under which most of them were used and equipped with safety devices to protect their occupants.

Now Chicago was behind him and he was heading north. One day he reached the river and knew exactly where he was. The old iron bridge, red with rust, still bridged the stream, and off to the east were the gray and weathered bones of a deserted village, and to the west, just short of the bridge, was an ancient track that flanked the river, running between the water and the limestone-ribbed, tree-covered bluffs.

Twenty miles, he thought—twenty miles was all and he would be home. Although, even as he thought about it, he knew it wasn't home and it had never been. It was simply familiar, a place he once had known.

He swung the car to the right and was on the river road, a narrow set of wheel tracks with a ribbon of grass between them and brush and drooping tree branches so close they rasped against the body of the car.

A hundred yards and the brush and trees ended and

137

ahead was a little meadow, which had been at one time, most likely, a cornfield or a pasture. Beyond the meadow the trees and brush closed in again. A short distance up the hillside a few tumbledown farm buildings sat amidst weeds and sprouting brush.

In the center of the clearing, just off the road, lay a camp. Dirty, patched tents stood in a circle. Thin spirals of blue smoke swirled up from cooking fires. Three or four battered, rusted cars stood to one side of the tents and there were animals which must have been horses, although Frost had never seen a horse. And there were dogs and people, all turned to look at him, some of them starting to move toward him and crying back and forth to one another—shrill, triumphant cries.

In the instant that it took for the scene to register upon Frost's mind, he knew what he had stumbled on—a band of Loafers, one of those strange and vicious tribes which roamed the countryside, that small percentage of unemployed and unemployable who through the years had resisted all attempts to find a place for them in the economic structure. There were not many of them, perhaps; but here was one of the bands and he'd run headlong into it!

He slowed the car, then changed his mind and accelerated, heading down the road, building up his speed in hope that he'd be able to run clear of the pack of humans who were streaming from the camp.

For a moment it seemed that he might have made it, for he pulled even with and was forging past the largest body of the running men. Looking out the window, to the side, he could see their screaming faces, bearded, dirty, mouths open in their shouting, lips peeled back to show their teeth.

Then suddenly the wave of charging bodies hit the car, ran into it as a man might run headlong into a fence, and it bounced alarmingly, hopping in the ruts, and then was going over, slowly tipping to one side, while the two wheels still in contact with the ground continued to give it some forward motion. And even as it tipped, the mass of screaming men swarmed onto it and forced it over.

It struck the ground and skidded, shuddering. Someone jerked open the door and hands reached in to haul Frost out. Once out, they dumped him on the ground. Slowly, he regained his feet. The Loafers ringed him like a pack of wolves, but now the viciousness was gone and there was amusement on their faces.

One man, standing in the forefront of the pack, nodded at him knowingly. "Now it was thoughtful," he said, "to deliver us a car. We sure God needed one. Our old ones are getting so they hardly run no more."

Frost did not answer. He glanced around the semicircle and all of them were laughing, or very close to laughing. Among the men were children, gangling little boys who stood and gawked at him.

"Horses are all right," said a slack-jawed man, "but they ain't as good as cars. They can't go as fast and they are a lot of trouble, taking care of them."

Frost still said nothing, mostly because he could not decide what might be safe to say. It was quite clear that these people meant to keep the car and there was nothing, he realized, that he could do about it. They were laughing now, at their own good fortune and his discomfiture, but at any moment, if he should say the word, he sensed they could turn ugly.

"Pa," a shrill boyish voice cried, "what is that there on his forehead? He has got a red mark there. What kind of thing is that?"

Silence fell. The laughter died. The faces took on grimness.

"An osty!" cried the slack-jawed man. "By God, he is an osty!"

Frost spun and made a sudden lunge. His hands grasped the upward side of the car and, with a single motion, he vaulted over it. He lit unsteadily on his feet and stumbled, saw the mob of Loafers pounding around each end of the car, closing in on him. He started a stumbling run and saw that he was trapped. The river lay in front of him and there was no chance of dodging to one side, for either way he turned the Loafers had him flanked. There was shouting and laughing once again, but it was vicious laughter, the shrill hooting of hysterical hyenas.

Stones whizzed past him and plunged into the ground or skipped through the grass and he hunched his shoulders to protect his head, but one caught him in the cheek and the blow of it jolted his whole body and it seemed for an instant that his head was coming off as swift pain lanced through his jaw and skull. A fog rose from the ground and obscured his vision and he was plunging into it and all at once, with no sense of having fallen, he was down and hands were reaching roughly for him and lifting and carrying him.

Through the haze of the fog and the deep rumble of the shouting voices, one bullhorn voice rang out loud and clear above all the rest of them. "Wait a minute, boys," it roared. "Don't throw him in just yet. He'll drown sure as hell if he has got his shoes on."

"Hell, yes," yelled another voice, "he has to have a chance. Get them shoes off him."

Someone was tugging at his shoes and he felt them leave his feet and he tried to yell out, but the best he could utter was a croak.

"Them pants of his will get waterlogged," yelled the man with the bullhorn voice.

And another said, "Them rescue boys might not even be able to fish him out should it happen he did drown."

Frost fought, but there were too many of them and his fight was feeble as they stripped him of his trousers and his jacket and his shirt and all the other clothes.

Then there were four men, one to each arm, one to each leg, and somewhere off to one side, someone was shouting out the count: "One! Two! Three!"

And each time at the count they swung him and at the count of three let go and he sailed out above the river, naked as a jaybird, and saw the river rushing up to meet him.

He struck sprawled out and spraddled out and the water hit him like a doubled fist. He sank into it, fighting and desperate and confused, down into the blue-greenness and the cold. Then he rose and broke the surface and worked his hands and feet, more by instinct than by purpose, to keep himself afloat. Something bumped hard against him and he flung out an arm to ward it off and felt the roughness of wood touch against his hide. He wound an arm around it and it floated and supported him and he saw that it was a drifting tree trunk, floating down the current. He swung himself around and got both arms over it and rested on it, looking back.

On the river's bank the Loafers pranced and hopped in a hilarious war dance, shouting out at him words he did not recognize and one of them, with an arm raised high, waved his trousers at him as if they might have been a scalp.

29

SOMETIME in the night the wind had blown down the cross again.

Ogden Russell sat up and rubbed the sleep out of his eyes.

He sat flat upon the sand and stared at the fallen cross and it was more, he thought, than a man should have to bear. Although, by now, he should be used to it. He had done everything he knew to keep the cross erect. He had hunted driftwood and had tried to brace and prop it. He had found some boulders at the water's edge and, with a great deal of work and time, had lugged them up the beach and with them formed a supporting circle at the cross's base. He had dug hole after hole in which to plant it and had used a heavy piece of driftwood as a tamper to pack the sand solidly about it.

But nothing worked.

Night after night, the cross fell down.

Might it be, he wondered, that this was no more than a persistent sign that he was not about to find the comfort and the faith he sought and that he might as well give up? Or might it be a testing of his worthiness to receive the boon he hunted?

And what were his shortcomings? Where had he failed?

He had spent long hours upon his knees, with the hot reflection of the running river water and sand scorching him, turning his hide into a peeling loathsomeness. He had wept and prayed and cried upon the Lord until his legs went dead from lack of circulation and his voice had grown hoarse. He had practiced endless spiritual exercises and he had allowed to flow out of him a yearning and a need that would melt a heart of stone. And he had lived entirely on the river clams and the occasional fish and the berries and

142

the watercress until his body had shrunk to skin and bones and his stomach ached with hunger.

Yet nothing happened.

There had been no sign.

God went on ignoring him.

And that was not all. He had used the last of the fuel from the two ancient pine stumps he'd found on the edge of the willow clump which grew back from the sandy beach. He had grubbed out the last of the roots that he could reach the day before and now all the fuel that he had left was the occasional piece of driftwood that he came across and the dead branches of the willows, which were largely worthless as fuel, burning out quickly to a fluffy ash.

And as if this were not enough of tribulation, there was the man in the canoe who, throughout the summer, had snooped about the river and at times had tried to talk with him, not seeming to understand that no proper and dedicated hermit ever talked with anyone.

He had fled from people. He had turned his back on life. He had come to this place where he'd be safe from both life and people. But the world intrudes even so, he thought, in the form of a man paddling a canoe up and down the river, perhaps spying on him, although why anyone should want to spy upon a poor and humble supplicant such as he, he could not well imagine.

Russell came slowly to his feet and, using both his hands, brushed the sand off his back and legs as well as he could manage.

He looked at the cross again and knew that he would have to do something better than he had been able to accomplish heretofore. The only answer, he told himself, was to swim ashore and find there a longer piece of driftwood to make a new upright for the cross and then sink it deeper in the sand. More deeply planted, it would not be so top heavy and might not tip so easily.

He walked across the sandbar to the river's edge and knelt there, dipping water with his two cupped hands to scrub his face. After he had washed, he stayed kneeling and looked out across the fog-misted plane of steel-gray water that moved with unhurried strength against the ragged background of the forest that crowded against the other shore.

143

He had done it right, he thought. He'd followed all the ancient rules of hermitry. He had come to a waste place of the earth, deep in the wilderness, and had isolated himself on this sandbar island in the middle of the river, where there was none or nothing to distract him. With his own hands he had made and reared the cross. He had nearly starved. He had followed proper form in his petitioning; he had wept and prayed, humiliating both the spirit and the flesh.

There was one thing. One single thing. And through all these weeks, he knew, he had fought from knowing it, from admitting it, from saying it. He had sought to keep it buried. He had tried to make himself forget it, make his mind and consciousness erase it.

But it came bobbing to the surface of his mind and there was no way to push it back. Here, in the quietness of this day which had yet to come to life, he was face to face with it.

The transmitter in his chest!

Could he seek for a spiritual eternity while he still clung to the promise of a physical eternity? Could he play at cards with God and have an ace tucked up his sleeve?

Must he, before his petition could be heard, get rid of the transmitter in his chest, turn himself back into a mortal man?

He sank forward on the beach, collapsing.

He could feel the moist sand grinding on his cheek and when he moved his lips, the corners of them collected little gobs of sand.

"Oh, God," he whispered in his fear and indecision, "not that, not that, not that . . ."

30

THE mosquitoes and the flies were bad and the packed earth of the wheel track that he walked in had been turned so hot by the sun that it burned the bare soles of his feet.

When he had finally paddled the floating tree trunk close enough to shore to reach solid land again, he had been forced to walk a half a mile or more through dense river bottom woods before he reached the road. In the process, he had encountered several nettle patches and, despite his attempts to skirt the plants, had been forced to walk through areas rank with poison ivy. The nettle rash still was full of fire, and the poison ivy blisters, he felt sure, would appear in a day or so. He faced rough times ahead.

For some miles he had feared the Loafers might come hunting him, but there had been no sign of them and by now he had come to the opinion that they were through with him. They had had their fun and there was nothing more that they asked of him. They had his car and clothing and all that he possessed and they'd tossed him in the river, hooting and whooping with delight, and that had been the end of it. They were not really vicious people. If they had been vicious, he'd likely not be here, walking doggedly down a wheel track, fighting off, with flapping hands, the mosquitoes and the flies, and itching almost unendurably from nettle stings.

He came to a creek, crossed by an old stone bridge, the rock of which it was built crumbling and scaling. Underneath it the creek ran sluggishly, only a few inches deep, over a bed of black alluvial mud.

Frost went on, crossing the bridge, following the grass-grown track, flailing with his hands to drive away the insect pests which swarmed all about him. But it seemed a hopeless task. He rubbed his hand across the back of his neck and it came away smeared red with blood from the squashed bodies of mosquitoes, so intent on feeding they had not tried to get away.

As the day wore on to evening, he knew it would be worse. When dusk fell the flies would disappear, but the mosquitoes then would rise in clouds from the swamps and sloughs in the bottomland. The few that feasted on him now were only a thin advance guard of those which would come when dusk had fallen.

When morning came he would be a mass of welts, his body sluggish with poison from the insect bites. More than likely his eyes would be swollen shut. He wondered vaguely if mosquitoes could finally kill a man.

If he could build a fire, the smoke would help protect him. Out on a sandbar in the river the prevalent river breeze would keep the pests thinned down. Or, possibly, if he could climb the bluffs and find a breezy hilltop he'd escape the worst of the hordes which would rise from the swamps once darkness fell.

He could not build a fire. And the thought of the climb to the bluff tops, or beating his way through the river bottoms back to the river's edge, left him shaken. The going would be rough and there would be poison ivy and there might be rattlesnakes and even if he reached the river he might not be able to reach a sandbar. The only sandbar might be far out and he was not too good a swimmer.

But he realized that he must do something. It already was late in the afternoon and he did not have much time.

He stood in the road, squinting up the bluffs, covered with trees and rank underbrush and weeds, capped by cliffs of rock.

There might be another way, he thought. Slowly the idea seeped into his brain. He turned about and went back to the bridge, clambering down the bank to the shallow stream. Stooping, he scooped up a handful of the mud. It was black and sticky and it smelled. He smeared the handful on his chest. He smeared it on his arms and shoulders. He plastered great handsful of it on his back. Then, working more carefully, he smoothed some of it on his face. The mud stuck to him and protected him. The shrill whine of the mosquitoes still sounded in his ears and they swarmed before his eyes, but they did not alight upon the mud smeared upon his body.

He went on smearing mud, covered his body as best he could. It seemed that the coolness of the mud, perhaps even some antiseptic quality in it, eased the itching and the pain of the mosquito welts and the nettle rash.

And here, he thought, he squatted, a naked savage on the bank of this muddy stream—far worse off than he had been back on the city streets. For now he had nothing, absolutely nothing. Here, almost at the end of the trail he had taken without knowing why he took it, he was finally beaten. He had held before a faint and far-off hope, but now there was no hope. He could not cope with the situation he now faced. He had no equipment and no knowledge that would enable him to meet it.

Perhaps, come morning, he should go back up the road to join the band of Loafers—if they still were there, if they would let him join them. It was not the kind of life he'd planned, but they might give him, at least, a pair of pants, perhaps a pair of shoes. There'd be food to eat and probably work to do.

More than likely, though, they'd drive him away as soon as he appeared. For he was an osty and no one, not even Loafers, were supposed to have any truck with osties. There was just the chance, however, that they wouldn't give a damn. They might let him join the tribe as a sort of whipping boy, as a tribal jester, for his entertainment value.

He shivered as he thought of it, that he should be so reduced in fortune and in pride as to be able even to think of it.

Or perhaps now was the time to take that one last road of desperation, to seek out the nearest monitor station and apply for death. And in fifty years, or a hundred or a thousand, to wake up again and be no better off than he was this moment. They would, of course, remove the marks of ostracism once he was revived, and he'd be a normal man again, but that would be all he'd be. They'd give him clothes to wear and he would stand in line for food and he'd have no dignity and no aspirations and no hope. But he'd have immortality—God, yes, he'd have immortality!

He rose and went questing up the stream to where he

had seen a few bushes loaded with blackberries. He picked and ate several handsful of them, then came back to his squatting place and sat down again. Idly, he dipped black mud from the bottom of the stream and did some repair work on his body.

It was quite clear that there was nothing he could do right now. Dusk already was creeping in and the mosquitoes swarmed about in clouds. He would have to spend the night here and in the morning he would have some more blackberries for breakfast and renew his coat of mud, then start out to do whatever it might be that he had to do.

Darkness fell and fireflies flickered out, dotting the bluffs and the heavy brush of the river bottomland with brief, tiny flecks of cold green fire. From somewhere in the tangle of the river forest a raccoon whickered. The east flushed with a golden light and the moon, almost full, arose. The whine of the mosquitoes filled every cranny of the night and a few got into his eyes and ears and he brushed them off. He dozed fitfully, waking each time with a start of terror, sometimes not knowing where he was, taking long seconds finally to orient himself. Little prowlers of the night came out and rustled all about him in the grass and weeds. A rabbit hopped down the road, stopped at the edge of the bridge, and stared solemnly down, its long ears tipped forward, at the strange figure huddled on the stream bank. Far away something barked with short, high, excited yips, and once, from the craggy cliffs atop the bluffs, a cat screamed, a sound that turned Frost's blood cold and set him to shivering.

He dozed and woke, dozed and woke again. And in his waking moments his mind, seeking to divorce itself from reality, went back to other days. To the man who had left the packages of food beside the garbage cans, to Chapman's visit when he was living in the cellar, to the old grizzled man who had asked if he believed in God and to that brief hour of candlelight and roses with Ann Harrison.

And why, he wondered, had that man fed him—a man he did not know, a man he'd never spoken with? Was there, he wondered, any sense at all in this life that mankind lived? Could there be any purpose in a life so senseless?

Sometime in the course of the long night he knew what he must do, realized, dimly and far off, a responsibility he had not known before. It did not come to him at once; it grew by slow degrees, as if it were a lesson learned most haltingly and very painfully.

He must not go back to the Loafers' camp. He must not ask for death. So long as he had life he must stay steadfast to a purpose that he did not know. He had started out to reach a certain farm, without knowing why, and he must go on until he reached his destination. For somehow it seemed that it was not he alone who was involved in this senseless journey, but Ann and Chapman and that strange man who'd asked him all the questions and the man who'd died out in the alley—or at least the memory of that man. He tried to make some sense out of all of this and it made no sense. But he knew that, in some way he could not fathom, he had become committed to a certain course and he must continue on that course regardless of all doubt.

Was it possible, he wondered, that this crazy compulsion to make the journey was the result of some sort of precognition that operated outside the normal mental process? Perhaps an added or extra function of the mind that worked only under stress and in a time of great emergency.

Morning finally came and he went up the creek to get more blackberries. Then he did a new and meticulous job with the mud again and started out.

Another fifteen miles or so and he'd come to the mouth of a certain hollow that ran down from the hills and by following up the hollow he'd finally reach the farm. He tried to recall how the mouth of the hollow looked and all that he could remember was that a short way up the hollow a spring gushed from the hillside and that a stream of water flowed through the culvert underneath the road and made its way into a little pond, choked by cattails and rank swamp growth. He'd have to rely on the spring and the creek as landmarks, he realized, for he could remember little else.

The nettle rash seemed to have worn itself out. The mosquitoes and the flies, balked by the mud, gave him little trouble.

He trudged along and the day wore on. His stomach grumbled at him and once, spying some mushrooms by the roadside, he stopped and eyed them, remembering that back in those days when he'd spent the summers on the farm he'd gone out with his grandfather to gather mushrooms. These looked like the ones they'd picked, but he could not be sure. Hunger and caution waged a battle and caution finally won and he went on down the road, without touching them.

The day grew hot and crows cawed in the river bottoms. Protected by the towering, bluff-crowned hills, the road had not a breath of breeze. Frost moved in a haze of heat and suffocating air, unstirred by any wind. The mud dried and flaked off his body or ran in dirty rivulets of sweat. But the mosquitoes now were fewer, retreating from the blazing sun to seek the roadside shade.

The sun reached midday height and slanted down the west. Great thunderheads towered in the west and the air went still. Nothing stirred and there was no sound of any sort. A sign of storm, Frost thought, remembering his grandmother and her weather signs.

For an hour or more he had been watching for landmarks that he might recognize, stopping every now and then at the top of a slight knoll to study the terrain ahead. But the road wound on through the everlasting walls of green, with scarcely anything to distinguish one mile from the next.

The day wore on and the clouds piled higher in the west. Finally the sun disappeared behind the clouds and the air became somewhat cooler.

Frost plodded on, one step and then another, and then another step—and it went on endlessly.

Suddenly he heard the sound of running water. He stopped and jerked up his head. And there the hollow was, with the running stream and the now-remembered configuration of the bluff looming to the right, with its great crown of limestone and the cedar trees growing from the ledge just below the top.

As if it were a place sprung full-bodied out of yesterday, it had a familiarity he had not expected. But despite the familiarity, there was a strangeness, too.

Something was hanging in a tree close beside the spring. There was a path beaten from the road up toward the spring and a sharp smell he could not recognize hung in the air.

Frost felt his body tensing as he stood there in the road and a sense of danger prickled at his scalp.

The sun by now was entirely hidden by the towering clouds and the recesses of the woods were dark and the mosquitoes were coming out again.

The thing hanging in the tree, he saw, was a knapsack, and the smell, he knew now, was the acrid odor of old, wet ashes. Someone had built a campfire by the spring and had gone off, leaving the knapsack hanging in the tree. Whether the campers had gone away for good or would be coming back, there was no way of knowing. But where there was a knapsack, there might possibly be food.

Frost turned off the road and padded cautiously up the path. He came out of the weeds that flanked the path and the little trampled area of the camp lay in front of him.

Someone, he saw, was there. A man lay upon the ground, on his side, with one leg doubled up almost to his belly and the other leg stretched out. Even from where he stood, Frost could see that the stretched-out leg was almost twice the size it should be, swelling out the fabric of the trouser leg so that it seemed to shine. The trouser leg was rolled up just above the ankle and beneath it the ballooning flesh was an angry red and black, puffed out beyond the fabric of the trouser and the shoe.

Dead, thought Frost. Dead and lying here how long? And that was strange, for a helicopter from a rescue station should long ago have picked up the body.

Frost moved forward and his foot caught a small branch that had fallen from a tree. The branch, with its half-dry leaves, made a rustling sound as he moved across it.

The man on the ground stirred weakly, trying to turn over on his back. His head turned to look in the direction of the noise and his face was a puffed-up mask. The eyes were swollen shut. The mouth moved, but there was no sound. Cracks ran across the lips and blood from the cracks had trickled down into the beard. The lips moved again and this time there was a croak.

The dead campfire was a mound of gray and beside it a small kettle lay upon one side.

Frost strode to the campfire, snatched up the kettle, hurried to the spring and came back with water.

He knelt and gently lifted the man, propped him with

his body. He lifted the water to his mouth and the man drank, slobbering and choking.

Frost took the kettle away and eased the man back on the ground.

A long rumble of thunder filled the valley and reverberated from the bluffs. Frost glanced up. Black clouds were boiling in the sky. The storm that had threatened all afternoon was about to break.

Rising, Frost went to the tree and took down the knapsack and opened it. A pair of trousers, a shirt, some socks, a few cans of food, some other odds and ends spilled out of it. A fishing rod was leaned against the tree.

He went back to the camper and the man pawed at him blindly. He lifted him and gave him more water, then let him down again.

"Snake," said the man. The sound was half word, half croak.

The thunder growled again. It was darker now.

Snake, the man had said. A rattlesnake, perhaps. With the country going back to wilderness, the rattlers would be on the increase.

"I'll have to move you," he told the man. "I'll have to carry you. It may hurt, but . . ."

The man did not answer.

Frost glanced at his face.

He looked like a man asleep. He had drifted off into a coma, probably. More than likely he'd been drifting in and out of one for hours, perhaps for days.

There was, Frost told himself, no second way about it. He had to carry the man to the farmhouse that sat atop the bluffs, get him under shelter, find some means to get him comfortable, build a fire, and get some warm food into him. The storm would break any minute now and he couldn't leave him exposed to its fury.

To make the trip he'd need the shoes the man was wearing and there were the trousers and the shirt that had fallen from the knapsack. Some food, too; he'd put a can or two of it in his pockets. And matches—he hoped there would be matches, or perhaps a lighter. He'd have to take the kettle along, tie it to his belt, perhaps. He'd need it when he warmed the food.

Two miles, he thought. At least two miles, and all uphill, over terrible terrain.

But it had to be done. A man's life was at stake.

The man mumbled and muttered.

"Want another drink?" asked Frost.

The man appeared not to have heard him.

"Jade," he mumbled. "Jade—a lot of jade . . ."

31

FRANKLIN CHAPMAN was sitting on the bench in front of the library, waiting, as he had waited every Wednesday and Saturday evening since that night he'd talked with Frost, when the first pain hit him. For a moment the streetlights and the lighted windows in the apartment house across the street, the blackness of the trees and the shining, light-streaked surface of the street shifted and revolved like a somber kaleidoscope as he doubled over with the flaming splash of fire that went through his chest and gut and arm.

He stayed huddled, arms wrapped tight around his belly, face lowered above the chest. He stayed quiet and the pain slowly drained from chest and gut, but the left arm still was numb and through the numbness throbbed a misery.

Cautiously, he straightened up and fear touched one corner of his brain, whispering a suspicion of what had caused the pain. He should go home, he thought, or better yet, flag down a cab and ask the driver to take him to the nearest hospital.

But he had to wait, he told himself, just a little longer. For he had said he'd wait, from nine to ten two evenings of the week. And what if Frost should need him?

Although there had been no sign or word of Frost since that night when the cook had been killed in the alley back of the restaurant. And Ann Harrison was gone, too, without a word to him that she was leaving.

What could have happened, he wondered, to the two of them?

He straightened carefully and laid the aching arm across his lap.

Funny how fuzzy he seemed to be. Just a little pain . . .

The pain hit him again and he doubled up.

Slowly he let out his sucked-in breath as the pain, after

154

its vicious stab, ebbed from his body to leave him limp and shaken.

I must not die, he told himself. Somehow I must keep from dying.

He clawed his way erect and stood hunched beside the bench. Down the street he saw the dome light of a cab. He ran, half stumbling, down the walk toward the street, waving his right hand at the oncoming cab.

The cab pulled in and the driver reached back to open the door. Chapman stumbled in, slumped into the seat. His breath was coming hard, whistling in his throat.

"Where to, mister?"

"Take me . . ." said Chapman, and stopped. For a sudden thought had struck him. Not to a hospital. Not immediately. There was another place that he must go first.

The cabbie was half turned in his seat, staring at him.

"Mister, are you all right?"

"I'm all right."

"You look a bit shook up."

"I'm O.K.," said Chapman. It was so hard to think. So hard to keep his thoughts straight. His mind was slow and muddy.

"I want to go," he said, "to a post office."

"There's one just down the street, but the windows will be closed."

"No," Chapman whispered. "Not just any post office. One particular one." He told the cabbie where it was.

The driver glanced at him suspiciously.

"Mister, you don't look so good to me."

"I'm all right," said Chapman.

He leaned back in the seat and watched the street slide past as the cab got underway. Most of the stores and shops were dark. A few lights still burned in the great hulks of the apartment houses. And just ahead was a church, with the burnished cross gleaming in the moonlight. Once, he remembered, he had gone to a church—for all the good it did him.

The night was quiet, and the city quiet, as it always was at night. He sat and watched it flow smoothly past him and there was in it, he found, a sort of peace. Earth and life, he thought, and both of them were good. The splashes of light that the lamps threw on the pavement, the padding cat, a part of the night itself, the painted signs advertising bargains, lettered on the windows of the shops—all these were things he'd seen before, but never really seen. And now, leaning back in the moving cab, he saw them for the first time, saw them as separate units which made up the city that he knew. Almost, he thought, as if he were saying good-by to all of it and was seeing it in an effort to remember it in the days when he'd be gone.

Although he was not going anywhere. First to the post office, then to a hospital, and when he reached the hospital he'd call home, for if he failed to call, Alice would worry, and she had enough to worry about without him adding to it. But no money worries. He felt good about that, thinking of the book and how she had no money worries.

The arm bothered him. He wished it would quit its aching. He felt all right now, except for the arm. A little weak and shaken, perhaps, but it was the arm that worried him.

The cab pulled up to the curb and the driver turned to open the door.

"Here we are," he said. "You want that I should wait?"

"If you please," said Chapman. "I'll be right out."

He climbed the steps haltingly, for it seemed to take a lot of effort. His legs seemed to drag and he was panting when he reached the top.

He crossed the lobby and found the box he'd rented weeks ago. The envelope, he saw, still was there—just one envelope.

B to F and back to A. He turned the knob slowly and carefully and it did not work. He spun the dial and did it once again and this time it opened. Reaching in, he took out the envelope and closed the box.

As he turned with the letter clutched in his hand, the pain struck at him once again—massive, brutal, terrible. Thundering blackness closed in upon him and he fell, not feeling the impact when his body hit the floor.

Moving in the hushed and glowing light of a brand-new dawn, the mind and consciousness of Franklin Chapman entered into the place called Death.

32

THE storm burst minutes after he had started out and, carrying the man cradled in his arms, Frost struggled through a land filled with the blinding slash of lightning, bursting with the clap and roll of thunder that reverberated back and forth among the hills, while rain sluiced down in torrents and the very ground beneath his feet seemed to crawl with the sliding movement of the runoff water gushing down the slope. Above him the trees thrashed like giant creatures in the agonies of death and high in the great cliffs that crowned the hills the wind moaned and howled in the silences between the crashing of the thunder.

The man he carried was no lightweight—a big and husky man—and there were many times that Frost had to stop to rest, lowering the man so that his weight rested on the ground while he still kept him cradled in his arms. In between the rests he fought his way, step by careful step, up the frightful steepness of the bluffside, the underfooting made soft and treacherous by the downpour. Below him he heard the vicious growling of the flood waters, funneled into the hollow off the hillsides and boiling down the steep, notched valley. By now, more than likely, the camp where he'd found the man he carried was under a foot or more of racing water.

A deep dusk had fallen with the coming of the storm and he could see only a few yards ahead of him. He had not dared to allow himself to think of the distance yet ahead. He thought no farther than the next step and then, when that had been taken, yet another step. Time ceased to have a meaning and the world became a few feet square and he moved forward in a fog of gray eternity.

Now, without any sign of coming to an end, the woods came to an end. One moment they were there, then he stepped out of them and before him stretched what once had been a hayfield, with the knee-high grasses slanting all one way before the fury of the wind, the white shine of their stems ghostly in the twilight, the spume of driven wind a solid mist above them.

Upon the hill above the field sat a house, a rock against the storm, surrounded by wind-lashed trees, and just above the near horizon a hump of darkness that must be the barn.

He trudged heavily out into the field and here the ground was not as steep and the nearness of the house put a spring into his step that he would have sworn was impossible.

He crossed the field and now, for the first time since he had started on the climb, he became aware of the warmth in the body that he carried. Climbing the hill it had been a burden only, a weight he had to support, that he had to carry. But now, once again, the weight became a man.

He went underneath the trees that stood around the house, while the lightning snarled through the skies and the surging wind beat at him with its freight of rain.

As he rounded the porch, the house took on its old familiar look. Even in the rain he could imagine the two rocking chairs close together on the porch and the two old people sitting in them of a summer evening, looking out across the river valley.

He reached the steps and they were rickety when he stepped on them, but they held his weight and he mounted to the porch.

And now the door, he thought. It had not occurred to him before, but now he wondered if it might be locked. But locked or not, he would get in—break in the door or break out a window. For the man he carried must be gotten under shelter.

He moved across the boards of the porch toward the door and as he neared it, the door came open and a voice said, "Put him over here."

The dark human figure moved ahead of him and he saw, against one wall, what appeared to be a cot.

Stooping, he laid the man on the cot and then stood erect. His arms were stiff and sore and it seemed that he could feel each muscle in them and for a moment the room swayed slightly, then was still.

The other person, the one who had opened the door, was

at a table on the other side of the room. A tiny tongue of light flickered, then grew bright and steady, and Frost saw that it was a candle. And the last time he had seen a candle had been that night (how long ago?) when Ann Harrison had sat across the table from him.

The other person turned and she was a woman—a plain, but forceful face, sixty maybe, perhaps more than that, an old face and yet in many ways an ageless face, calm and confident. She wore her hair skinned back into a bun that rode low on her neck and she wore a ragged sweater that had an elbow hole.

"What is wrong with him?" she asked.

"Snakebit. I found him, alone, in a camp down on the river road."

She picked up the candle and came across the room to hand it to him.

"You hold this," she said, "so I have some light to work by."

She bent above the man on the cot.

"It's his leg," said Frost.

"I can see," she said.

She reached out her hands and laid hold of the tattered bottom of the trouser leg. Her hands jerked apart and the fabric ripped with a screeching sound. She took hold of the edges of the torn cloth and jerked them again and the cloth fell away, leaving the leg exposed.

"Hold the light lower," she told him.

"Yes, ma'am," said Frost.

The flesh of the leg was splotched, black with angry red spots here and there. The skin, stretched tight by the swelling, glistened in the candlelight. A few open sores seeped pus.

"How long has he been like this?"

"I don't know. I found him this afternoon."

"You packed him up the hill? In this storm?"

"There was no way out of it," he said. "I had to."

"There's not much I can do," she said. "We can get him cleaned up. Some hot soup into him. Keep him comfortable."

"There's no medical aid available, of course."

"There's a rescue and monitor station about ten miles from here," she said, "and I have a car. We can take him

159

there when the storm stops. But the road is too bad to try it while it still is storming. There's too much danger of washouts and there are apt to be some bad mudholes. If we can get him there, they'll fly him into Chicago with a helicopter."

She turned about and started for the kitchen. "I'll poke up the fire," she said, "and heat some water. You can try to get him cleaned up a bit while I cook some soup. We'll try to get some down him."

"He talked to me a bit," said Frost. "Not much. Something crazy about a lot of jade. It was like carrying a dead man. I think he was out cold most of the time I carried him. But I knew he was still alive because of the body heat."

"It would be a bad time," she said, "for a man to die. And a bad place. Even more so down there in the valley. In a storm like this, the rescue unit would never get to him in time."

"I thought of that," said Frost.

"You came straight here. You knew there was a house?"

"Many years ago," he said, "I knew about the house. I did not expect to find it occupied."

"I've been using it," she said. "I didn't think anyone would mind."

"I'm sure no one will," he said.

"You look as if you could use some food yourself," she told him, "and some rest."

"There is something, ma'am," he said, "that I have to tell you. I'm an osty. I've been ostracized and I'm not supposed to talk with anyone and no one is supposed . . ."

She lifted a hand. "I know what ostracism is. There's no need to explain."

"What I mean to say is, it's only fair to tell you. You can't tell in bad light. I let my beard grow and it hides the worst of the marks. I'll stick around and help you with the man if you want me to and then I'll get out. I don't want to get you into any sort of trouble."

"Young man," she said, "ostracism doesn't mean a thing to me. I doubt it does to anyone out here in the wilderness."

"But I don't want . . ."

"And if you're ostracized and not supposed to have anything to do with anyone, why did you bother with this man?"

"I couldn't leave him there. I couldn't let him die."

"You could," she said. "Ostracized, he was no concern of yours."

"But ma'am ..."

"I've seen you somewhere before," she said. "Without the beard. I thought so the first time I saw your face in the candlelight, but ..."

"I don't think you did," he said. "My name is Daniel Frost and ..."

"Daniel Frost, of Forever Center?"

"That is right. But how ..."

"The radio," she told him. "I have a radio and I listen to the news. They said you'd disappeared. They said there'd been some sort of scandal. They never said you'd been ostracized. Later there was an item about some murder and ... but I know now where I saw you. It was at the New Year's party just a year ago."

"The New Year's party?"

"The one at Forever Center in New York. You may not remember me. We were not introduced. I was with the Timesearch project."

"Timesearch!" he almost shouted. For he knew now who this woman was. The one who B.J. said must be found, the one who'd disappeared.

"I'm glad to finally meet you, Daniel Frost," she said. "My name is Mona Campbell."

33

ANN HARRISON knew now that once again she had wandered into a dead-end road, but there was little she could do about it except to go on until she found a place she could turn the car around. Then she would retrace her way and try for another road that would lead her west.

Once, long ago, the roads had been numbered and well marked and there had been maps available at any service station. But now the road markers had mostly disappeared and there were no service stations. With cars powered by long-life storage batteries, there was no longer any need of service stations.

Out here in the wilderness it was a matter of making out the best one could, ferreting out the roads that would take one where he wished to go, making many wrong turnings, backtracking to find another way—some days making only a few miles on one's route and seldom being sure of where one really was. Occasionally there were people who could be asked, occasionally there were towns that could be identified. But other than this, it was a matter of good guessing.

The day was warm and the heavy growth that grew close against the road to make a tunnel of it trapped and held the heat. Even with the windows open, it was hard to breathe.

The road had grown narrower in the last mile or so and now was little more than a dugout sliced into the hillside. To the right the hill rose steeply, dense and thick with trees and underbrush, with gray boulders, splotched with moss, poking from the leaf-covered earth beneath the trees. To the left the ground sloped sharply away, studded with boulders and with trees.

Ann made a bargain with herself. If, within another five minutes of driving she did not find a place to turn around, she would back the car to the fork she had taken several miles back. But it would be slow work and perhaps even hazardous because of the narrowness of the track, and she didn't want to do it unless it was necessary.

Ahead of the car tree branches arched and met to make the road a tunnel and some of the branches, drooping low, or leaning out from the side of the road, brushed against the car.

She saw the nest too late, and even seeing it, did not recognize it for what it was. It was a gray ball that looked like a wad of dirty paper hanging from one of the branches that scraped, at windshield height, against the side of the car.

It scraped around the windshield post and bounced suddenly into the open window and as it swung it erupted in a blur of buzzing insects.

And in that instant Ann recognized the wadded ball of paper—a wasp nest.

The insects exploded in her face and swarmed into her hair. She screamed and threw up her hands to fight them off. The car lurched and seemed to stagger, then plunged off the road. It smashed into one tree, bounced off, slammed into a boulder and caromed around it, finally came to rest, still upright, its rear end wedged between two trees.

Ann found a door handle and pushed down on it. The door came open and she threw herself out, rolling off the edge of the seat and hitting the ground. She scrambled to her feet and ran, wildly, blindly. She slapped at her face and neck. She tripped and fell and rolled, was brought up by a fallen tree trunk.

One wasp was crawling on her forehead, another buzzed angrily in her hair. There were two painful, burning areas on the back of her neck and another on her cheek.

The wasp on her forehead flew away. Slowly she sat up and shook her head. The buzzing ceased. That wasp, too, apparently was gone.

She pulled herself to her feet, became aware of many bruises and abrasions and a few more stings. There was a muted throbbing in one ankle. She sat down carefully on the fallen tree trunk and beneath her weight rotted wood crumbled and fell away, dropping to the forest floor.

Around her the wilderness was black and gray and green

—and the silence green as well. Nothing stirred. It waited. It crouched and was sure of itself. It did not care.

She felt the mental scream rise in her brain and fought it down. This was no time, she told herself, to give way to nerves. The thing to do was to stay for a moment on this log and get her thoughts together, to make assessment of the situation and then go up the hill and see what shape the car was in. Although she was sure that the car, even if it were in operating order, would not, under its own power, pull itself back onto the road. Cars were built for city streets, not for terrain such as this.

It had been foolish to start out, of course. This was a trip she never should have tried. She had started, she remembered, driven by two motives—the need to escape the surveillance by Forever Center and in the faint belief that she knew where Daniel Frost might be.

And why Daniel Frost? she asked herself. A man she had seen but once, a man she had cooked a dinner for and eaten with at a table set with candles and red roses. A man she had found easy to talk with. A man who had promised help even when he knew that he had no help to give, even when he faced some terrible danger of his own. And a man who had said he spent his boyhood summers at a farm near Bridgeport in Wisconsin.

And a man who later had been made a pariah.

Lost dogs, she thought, and homeless cats—although there were no longer many dogs or cats. And lost causes. She was a sucker for lost causes, an inevitable and unremitting champion of misfortune. And what had it gotten her?

It had gotten her this, she thought. Here in the depths of an unknown woods, on a dead-end, dying road, hundreds of miles from anywhere or anyone who counted—bee-stung and bruised and something wrong with one ankle and a complete damn fool.

She pulled herself erect and stood for a moment, testing the ankle. While there was some pain, she found that it would support her.

She walked slowly up the hill. Her feet sank into the black loam carpeted by the dead leaves which represented the falls of many years. She dodged around boulders and, reaching out, grasped at saplings and hanging branches to help herself along.

Occasionally an angry wasp went thrumming past, but the swarm appeared to have settled down.

She reached the car and one glance told her that it was useless. A wheel had struck a boulder squarely and was crumpled.

She stood and looked at it and thought what she must do.

Her sleeping bag, of course—it was light in weight, but a little bulky for easy carrying. As much food as she could manage and the hatchet to cut wood for fires, some matches, an extra pair of shoes.

There was no use staying here. Somewhere, on one of those wild, abandoned roads, she would find some help. Somehow she would work it out. And once she'd worked it out, what would she do then? She had only come a few hundred miles and there were many more to go. Should she continue on her crazy odyssey or go back to Manhattan and Forever Center?

A sound jerked her around—the soft scraping sound of wood brushing against metal and the faint humming that could only be an electric motor.

Someone was driving down the road! Someone trailing her?

Fear flowed over her and her strength and bravery deserted her and she sank into a crouch, huddling there beside her wrecked car, while the other car, screened from her sight by the heavy foliage, crept slowly down the road.

It must be someone who had followed her, she told herself. For this was a road that seemed to lead to nowhere, a steadily worsening road that in a little while, more than likely, would dwindle down to no road at all.

In just a few more seconds the car would reach the wasp nest and what would happen then? The insects would not take such a disturbance lightly. Stirred up by their first encounter, they would come swarming out bent upon full vengeance.

The noise of the branches and the brush scraping against the metal of the car came to an end. The electric motor was humming idly. The car had stopped before it reached the nest.

A door banged and leaves rustled under the scuffing of deliberate footsteps. The footsteps stopped. The silence stretched out thin. The footsteps began, then stopped again.

A man cleared his throat, as if he'd been about to speak and then had decided not to.

The feet upon the road stirred about—not footsteps, but indecisive shuffling.

A voice spoke tentatively, a normal speaking voice, as one might speak who was reluctant to break the woodland spell.

"Miss Harrison," asked the voice, "are you anywhere about?"

She half raised out of the crouch, surprised. She had heard that voice somewhere and she should know it—and suddenly she did.

"Mr. Sutton," she said, as calmly as she could, determined not to shout, not to sound excited, "I'm down here. Watch out for the wasp nest."

"What wasp nest?"

"There's one on the road. Just ahead of you."

"You're all right?"

"Yes, I'm all right. Stung up a little. You see, I drove into the nest and the car went off the road and . . ."

She forced herself to stop. The words were coming out too fast, gushing out. She had to hang onto herself. She must fight off hysteria.

He was off the road now, plunging down the hill toward her. She saw him coming—the big, blunt man with the grizzled face.

He stopped and stared at the car.

"Busted up," he said.

"One wheel is broken. Just caved in."

"You ran me quite a chase," he said.

"But why—how did you find me?"

"Just dumb luck," he said. "There are a dozen of us out looking for some trace of you. Covering different areas. And I was the one to pick up your trail. A day or two ago. When you talked to some people in a village."

"I stopped several times," she said, "to ask my way."

He nodded. "Then there was the house up by the fork. They told me you went this way. Said the road petered out. Said you'd get in trouble on it. No proper road at all."

"I didn't see a house."

"Maybe not," he said. "It sets back from the road a piece.

Up on a knoll. Not an easy thing to see. Dog came out, barking at me. That is how I knew."

She rose to her feet.

"Now what?" she asked. "Why come after me?"

"We need you. There is something that you have to do. Something that we can't do. Franklin Chapman's dead."

"Dead!"

"Heart attack," he said.

"The envelope!" she cried. "He was the only one who knew . . ."

"It's all right," he said. "We have the envelope. We'd been keeping tab on him. A cabdriver picked him up and took him to a post office . . ."

"That's where the letter was," she said. "I asked him to rent a box under an assumed name and I gave him the envelope and he mailed it to himself and left it in the box. A legal maneuver. So I wouldn't know where the letter was."

"The cabbie was one of us," said Sutton. "One way we kept track of him. Looked sick when he got into the cab and . . ."

"Poor Franklin," she said.

"He was dead when he hit the floor. Never knew what happened."

"But there's no second life for him, no . . ."

"A better second life," said Sutton, "than Forever Center plans."

34

FROST sat on the steps that led down from the porch and stared out across the valley. The first shadow of evening had fallen on the river and the bottomlands and above the far-off treetops a straggly line of black forms flew raggedly, a flock of crows heading back to their nesting grounds. On the far side of the river a small white ribbon ran like a snake across the rounded hills, the track of an ancient and abandoned road.

Down the slope below him stood the barn, its ridgepole sagging, and beside it the rusted hulk of a piece of farm machinery. At the far end of the long-fallow field a dark form went leaping through the tall grass, a wild dog, more than likely, possibly a coyote.

Once, he remembered, the lawn had been mowed and the bushes trimmed and the flower beds pampered. Once, in his own memory, the fences had been kept in repair and painted, but now all the paint was gone and half of the fence was gone. The front gate hung drunkenly on a single hinge, half pulled from the post.

Outside the gate stood Mona Campbell's car, the tall grass and weeds reaching halfway to the windows and hiding the wheels. It was an incongruous note, he thought. It had no right to be here. Man had fled from this land and now it should be left alone, it should be allowed to rest from man's long tenancy.

Behind him the door closed softly and footsteps came across the porch. Mona Campbell sat down on the step below him.

"It is a pleasant view," she said. "Don't you find it so?"

He nodded.

"I suppose you remember many pleasant days in this place."

"I suppose I do," said Frost, "but it was so long ago."

"Not so long ago," she told him. "Only twenty years or less."

"It's empty. It's lonesome. It is not the same. But I'm not surprised. That's the way I expected it."

"But you came," she said. "You ran for shelter here."

"I came because I had to. Something made me come. I don't pretend to understand what it was that made me, but that's the way it was."

They sat in silence for a moment and he saw that her hands lay idly and quietly in her lap—hands that had some wrinkles in them, but still small and capable. At one time, he thought, those hands had been beautiful, and in a certain way, they had not lost their beauty yet.

"Mr. Frost," she said, without looking at him, "you didn't kill that man."

"No," he said, "I didn't."

"I didn't think you had," she said. "You have nothing to run for except the marks upon your face. Has it occurred to you that you might reinstate yourself if you turned me in?"

"The thought," said Frost, "had crossed my mind."

"You considered it?"

"Not really. When you're driven in a corner, you think of everything. You even think of things you know you couldn't do. But in this instance, of course, it would have been no good."

"I think it might," she said. "I would imagine they want me pretty bad."

"Tomorrow," Frost finally said, "I'll be leaving. You're in trouble enough without my adding to it. After all, I've had a week of rest and food and it's time to be getting on. It might not be a bad idea if you moved on, too. No one on the lam can afford to sit too long."

"There is no need," she said. "There is no danger. They don't know. How could they know?"

"You took Hicklin to the rescue station."

"At night," she said. "They never really got a look at me. Told them I was driving through and found him on the road."

"That's true enough," he said. "But you're forgetting Hicklin. The man could talk."

"I don't think so. He was delirious most of the time, remember. When he talked, he didn't know what he was saying. All that talk about some jade."

"So," he said, "you aren't going back to Forever Center. You're never going back?"

"I'm not going back," she said.

"What are you going to do?"

"I don't know," she said. "But I'm not going back. It's unreal back there. It's a fantasy—a hard, cruel fantasy. Once you've touched reality, once you've felt the reality of the naked land, once you've lived with dawn and sunset . . ."

She turned sidewise on the step and looked fully at him. "You don't understand, do you?"

He shook his head. "It may not be the way to live," he said. "I think we all know that. But we're working toward another life and that's important, I believe. It may not be the right way to do it. In other generations, we'll find better ways. But we make out the best we can . . ."

"Even after what has happened to you, you still can say this? After you were framed and railroaded into ostracism, even after they tried to frame you with a murder, you still can believe in Forever Center?"

"What happened to me," he told her, "must have been the work of a few men. It doesn't mean that the principles on which Center is based are wrong. I have as much reason and as great a right to subscribe to those principles as I ever did."

"I have to make you understand," she said. "I don't know why it is so important, but I have to make you understand."

He looked at her—the intense, old-maidish face with the hair skinned back tight into its bun, the thin, straight lips, the colorless eyes, the face lighted by some inner glow of human dedication that seemed entirely out of place. A schoolteacherish face, he thought, masking a mind as sharp and methodical as a thousand-dollar watch.

"Perhaps," he said, softly, "the understanding lies in what you haven't told me and what I haven't asked."

"You mean why I ran away. Why I took my notes."

"That would be my guess," he said. "But you needn't tell me. Once I would have wanted you to tell me; now it doesn't seem to matter."

"I ran away," she said, "because I wanted to make sure."

"That what you'd found was right?"

"Yes, I suppose that's it. I'd held off making any kind of progress report and the time was coming when I had to make one and—how do I say this?—I would imagine that in certain rather important things you have a tendency to say nothing, to give no hint of what you think you've learned until you're absolutely sure. So I panicked—well, not really panicked. I thought that if I could go off by myself for a while . . ."

"You mean you left, intending to come back?"

She nodded. "That is what I thought. But now I can't go back. I found out too much. More than I thought I'd find."

"That traveling back in time involves more than we thought it might. That it . . ."

"Not more than we thought it might," she said. "Really, there's nothing at all involved. And the answer's very simple. Time travel is impossible."

"Impossible!"

"That's right—impossible. You can't move in time or through time or around it. You can't manipulate it. It's too firmly interwoven into what you might call a universal matrix. We are not going to be able to use time travel to take care of our excess population. We either colonize other planets or we build satellite cities out in space or we turn the earth into one huge apartment house—or we may have to do all these things. Time was the easy way, of course. That's why Forever Center was so interested . . ."

"But are you sure? How can you be sure?"

"Mathematics," she said. "Non-human math. The Hamal math."

"Yes, I know," he said. "I was told you were working with it."

"The Hamalians," she said, softly, "must have been strange people. An entirely logical people who were much concerned, not only with the surface phenomena but the basic roots of the universe. They dug into the fact and the purpose of the universe and to do this they developed mathematics that they used not only to support their logic but as logic tools."

She reached out a hand and laid it on his arm. "I have a feeling," she said, "that eventually they'd arrived at final

171

truth—if there is such a thing as final truth. And I believe there must be."

"But other mathematicians . . ."

"Yes, other mathematicians used the Hamal math. And were puzzled by it, for they viewed it only as a system of formal axioms. They saw only symbols and formulas and statements. They used it as a physical expression and it is more than that . . ."

"But this means that we will have to wait," he cried. "It means some of the people in the vaults must wait. Must wait until we can build a place—or many places—for them, until we can find other solar systems with earthlike planets. And the planets are there, of course, but they're all like Hamal IV. They have to be terraformed and while we are terraforming them, the population will keep on expanding."

He looked at her with terror in his eyes. "We'll never catch up," he said.

They never would catch up. They had waited far too long. They had waited because immortality had seemed within their grasp. And they had waited because they could afford to wait, because they had all the space they needed once they had cracked time travel—and now time was out of reach.

"Time is one of the factors of the universal matrix," Mona Campbell said. "Space is another factor and matter/energy is the third. They're all bound together, woven together. They can't be separated. They can't be destroyed. We can't manipulate them."

"We got around the Einstein limitations," said Frost. "We did what everyone had believed could not be done. Perhaps we can . . ."

"Perhaps," she said, "but I don't think so."

"You don't seem to be upset about it."

"There is no need to be," she said. "I haven't told you all of it. Life is a factor, too. Perhaps I should say life/death, in the same sense that we say matter/energy, although I imagine the analogy is not exactly right."

"Life/death?"

"Yes, like matter/energy. You might call it, if you wished, the law of the conservation of life."

He got up shakily from the steps and went down them to

the ground. He stood for a moment, looking out across the valley, then turned back to her again.

"You mean that we went to all this trouble, all this work, for nothing?"

"I don't know," she said. "I've tried to think it out, but I don't have the answer yet. Perhaps I never will. All I know is that life is not destroyed, it is not quenched or blown out like a candle flame. Death is a translation of this property that we call life to another form. Just as matter is translated into energy or energy into matter."

"Then we do go on and on?"

"Who are we?" she asked.

And that is right, he thought. We *are* we?

A mere dot of consciousness that stood up in arrogance against the vastness and the coldness and the emptiness and the uncaring of the universe? A thing (a thing?) that thought it mattered when it did not matter? A tiny, flickering ego that imagined the universe revolved around it— imagined this when the universe did not know that it existed, nor cared that it existed?

And that kind of thinking, he told himself, could have been justified at one time. But not any longer. Not if what Mona Campbell said was true. For if what she said was true, then each little flickering ego was a basic part of the universe and a fundamental expression of the purpose of the universe.

"One thing," he said. "What are you going to do about it?"

She shook her head, bewildered now that the question had been asked. "What would happen, do you think, if I published my calculations? What would happen to Forever Center? To the people, both the living and the dead?"

"I don't know," he said.

"What could I tell them?" Mona Campbell asked. "No more than I've told you. That life goes on, that it can't be destroyed, no more than energy. That it's as everlasting as time and space itself. Because it is one with time and space in the fabric of the universe. I couldn't hold out any hope or promise beyond the certainty that there is no end to life. I couldn't say to them that death might be the best thing that could happen to them."

"But it could, of course."

173

"I rather think it could."

"But someone else, twenty years from now," he said, "fifty years from now, a hundred years—someone will find what you have found. Forever Center is convinced that you found something. They know you were working with the Hamal math. They'll put a team to work on it. Someone's bound to find it."

Mona Campbell sat quietly on the step. "That may be," she said. "But they'll be the ones to tell them, not I. I can't, somehow, see myself as the one who tears down everything the race has built in the last two hundred years."

"But you'd be replacing it with new hope. You'd confirm the faith that mankind held through many centuries."

"It's too late for that," she said. "We're fashioning our own immortality, our own foreverness. We have it in our hands. You can't ask mankind to give up something like that for . . ."

"And this is why you're not going back. Not because you shrink from telling us time travel is impossible. But because once we know it's impossible, we'll find out about life going on forever."

"That's it," she told him. "I can't make mankind into a pack of fools."

35

OGDEN RUSSELL stopped his digging when he hit what he thought to be a rock. All he had to dig with was his hands and the hole was not deep enough and the cross that had plagued him all these days—that cross would beat him yet.

He straightened in the hole, which reached halfway between knee and hip, and looked at the cross stretched upon the ground, the cross piece now affixed by the lengths of grapevine to the longer piece of driftwood he'd found on shore and towed across the river.

There was no question that he had too long an upright that required too deep a hole. A shorter one would have been far better. But there had been little choice; he'd taken what he found. And he had no saw or ax he could use to shorten it.

To hold the cross erect, as now constructed, the hole would have to be twice the depth it was. And now he'd have to start all over at another place, several feet removed, because even if he could dig around the rock, there'd be no way to haul it from the hole.

He leaned wearily against the wall of the hole and pounded petulantly at the rock with a bare heel and as he pounded at it, he became aware that the rock did not seem as hard as a rock should be.

He stopped the pounding and leaned there thinking of the strange non-hardness of the rock, and as he thought about it, he remembered something else, that the rock had seemed far smoother than was the case with the usual rock.

He shook his head in puzzlement.

It might not be a rock and if it was not a rock, then what could it be?

He squatted down into the hole again, his body cramped in its close confines and ran his hands over the hardness at

175

its bottom, and he had been right. The rock was smooth. He put a palm against it and pushed and it seemed to him there was a strange sense of resiliency to the smoothness at the bottom of the hole.

Mystified and excited, he dug several handsful of sand out of one side of the hole and found that he could dig below the level of the rock.

He dug some more and his fingers found the edge of the smooth hardness and wrapped themselves around it. He jerked, putting as much power as his cramped position would permit into the effort. The thing he'd thought of as a rock peeled back and upward and he saw it was not a rock, but metal, eroded and pitted and flaking off in tiny specks of brown-red pieces, the old rusted bits of metal that had stayed intact until this moment of disturbance.

Beneath the peeled-back piece of metal was a cavity, half filled with drifted sand, but with objects, wrapped in what appeared to be yellowed paper, thrusting from the sand.

Russell reached down and snatched up one of the paper-wrapped objects. The paper was old and brittle and crumpled at his touch. When he stripped it off, he held in his hand an object carved in an intricate design.

Straightening up and holding out his hand in the full light of the sun, he saw what he had—a piece of carved jade, shaped most cunningly. The blue-green of the base was the water from which the white jade carp arose, with each scale graved in delicate perfection. The workmanship was exquisitely performed and Russell's hand, holding the carving, trembled as he looked at it.

Here was beauty, here was treasure, here, if each of the paper parcels held another piece of jade, was a fortune such as few men ever dreamed.

Carefully he set the carving on the sand outside the hole and quickly bent down to come up with other parcels. In the end, spread out on the sand before him, were more than two dozen of the carvings done in jade.

He looked at them, laid out in solemn rows, and his eyes were misted and tears ran down the stubble of his cheeks.

For weeks he had begged and pleaded, for weeks he'd eaten out his heart with anguish and had fed on clams, which he detested, and all the time, in the sand beneath his feet this treasure had rested, an unexpected and mysterious cache which had waited to be found, for how long no man knew, until he had begun to dig this deeper hole to erect a better cross.

Treasure, he thought. Not the treasure he had sought, but undeniably a treasure and the kind of treasure which would make it possible for a man to enter on his second life on a sound financial footing.

He clambered from the hole and squatted by the jade, staring at it, occasionally reaching out a finger to prod at a certain piece, unable to convince himself that he had really found it.

A treasure, he thought. One he had not sought, but one which he had found while he had sought yet another, perhaps less substantial, treasure.

Was this, he wondered, yet another testing, one with the clams, one with all the discomfort and frustration and misery he had suffered on this island? Had the carvings been placed here, by some method he could not comprehend, to determine whether he might be worthy of that other treasure?

Perhaps he was wrong in hesitating. Perhaps he should snatch up all the carvings and heave them far out into the river as a sign that he renounced all worldly things. And having done that, go back to the digging of the hole so he could plant a cross that would not be blown over by the wind. And after that, perhaps, as a further evidence of faith, rip the transmitter from his chest and also throw it in the river, thus to strip himself of everything that bound him to the world?

He huddled on the sandbar and rocked back and forth, hands clasped around his middle, in the depth of misery.

Would there be no end to it? he asked himself. Would there ever be an end? Was there no limit to the debasement that a man must heap upon himself?

God was kind and merciful—the books all said He was. He yearned to win the souls of men and bind them close to Him. And the way was always open, the road was always clear—all one needed was to travel it to reach eternal glory.

But on this island there had been no mercy. There had been no sign and no encouragement. No road had been revealed and the jade had been in a rusted container of some sort of metal and that would not be the way of it had it been planted by divine intervention.

After all, he asked himself, why should God put Himself to the bother necessary to achieve such intervention? Why should He bother with him, at all? With him, one silly, stupid man when there were so many billion others. Why had he expected it? How could he have expected it? Was not the very fact he had expected it a sign of vanity, which was in itself a sin?

He reached out and picked up one of the pieces tight inside his fist and lifted it and cocked his arm to throw. Sobs shook him and his beard was soaked with tears already shed.

He cocked his arm to throw and he could not throw. His tightened fist came open and the jade slid from it and fell upon the sand.

And in that awful moment he knew that he had lost, that he was wanting in that essential capacity for humility that would unlock the gates of understanding he had sought so earnestly and, now it seemed apparent, priced at a cost too high—a cost that his basic brute humanity would never let him pay.

36

MONA CAMPBELL had left, sometime in the night. The car was gone and there were no tire tracks in the dew-wet grass. And she would not be back, for the coat that had hung on the hook behind the kitchen door was gone and there were no other clothes. The house was bare of anything that could bear testimony she ever had been there.

Now the house seemed empty; not empty because there was no one in it, but empty in the sense that it no longer was a structure meant for human habitation. It belonged to another time, another day. Man had no further use for houses such as this, set in the midst of empty acres. Today men lived in towering blocks of masonry and steel that stood huddled in places where there was no empty ground. Man, who once had been a wanderer and at times a loner, now had joined a pack and in the days to come there would be no separate houses and no separate structures. Rather, the entire world would be a single structure and its swarming billions would live deep underground and high up in the sky. They'd live in floating cities that rode the ocean's surface and in massive domes on the ocean's floor. They'd live in great satellites that would in themselves be cities, circling out in space. And the time would come when they'd go to other planets that had been prepared for them. They'd use space wherever they could find it and they'd achieve other space when there was no more to find. And they would have to do this, for space was all they had. The dream of fleeing into time was dead.

Frost stood on the porch and stared across the weed-grown, rushy wilderness that once had been a farm. The old fence row had grown into a windbreak, trees rearing tall into the sky where there had been brush and saplings when he had been a boy and come here for vacations. The fences were broken and sagging and the day was not far off when there would be no fences. And in another century, with no one to care for them or keep them in repair, the house and barn might be gone as well, disappearing gradually into a moldering pile of timbers.

Mona Campbell was gone and now he'd be going, too. Not that he had anywhere to go, but simply because there was no point in staying here. He'd go walking down the road and he'd wander aimlessly, for there would be no purpose in his going. He'd live off the land. He would manage somehow and he'd probably wander south, for in a few more months this country would grow cold and snow would fall.

Southwest, perhaps, he thought. To the desert country and the mountains, for that was a place he had often thought he would like to see.

Mona Campbell was gone and why had she gone? Because, perhaps, she feared that he might betray her in the hope he might be reinstated as a human being. Or, perhaps, because she knew now she should not have told him what she did and through the telling of it now felt that she was vulnerable.

She had fled, not to protect herself, but to protect the world. She walked the lonely road because she could not bear to let mankind know it had been wrong for almost two centuries. And because the hope she had found in the Hamal math was too poor and frail a thing to stand up against the elaborate social structure man himself had forged.

The Holies were right, he thought—as mankind itself had been right for many centuries in the faith it held. Although, he knew, the Holies would reject out of hand the evidence of life's foreverness because it held no promise of everlasting glory, nor the sound of silver trumpets.

For it promised nothing beyond life going on into eternity. It did not say what form that life would take or even if it would have a form. But it was evidence, he thought, and that was better than mere faith, for faith was never more, even at the best, than the implied hope for evidence.

Frost came down off the porch and started across the

yard, toward the sagging gate. He could go anywhere he wished and he might as well get started. There was no packing to be done and no plans to make, for everything he had was the clothes upon his back—the clothes that once had belonged to a man named Amos Hicklin—and without a purpose, there was no sense in making plans.

He had reached the gate and was pulling it open when the car came down the road, breaking suddenly out of the woods that grew close up to the house.

He stood astonished, with his hand upon the gate, and the first thing that he thought was that Mona Campbell had come back, that she'd forgotten something, or had changed her mind, and was coming back again.

Then he saw there were two people in the car and that the both of them were men and by that time the car had pulled up before the gate and stopped.

A door of the car came open and one of the men stepped out.

"Dan," said Marcus Appleton, "how good to find you here. And especially when we were least expecting you."

He was affable and jolly, as if they were good friends.

"I suppose," said Frost, "I could say the same of you. There've been times I've expected you to come popping out at me, but surely not today."

"Well, that's all right," said Appleton. "Any time at all. That suits me just fine. I had not expected I'd bag the two of you."

"The two?" asked Frost. "You're talking riddles, Marcus. There is no one here but me."

The driver had gotten out of the other door and now came around the car. He was a big man and he had a face that squinted and he wore a big gun on his hip.

"Clarence," said Appleton, "go on in the house and bring out the Campbell gal."

Frost came through the gate and stood aside so Clarence could go through it. He watched the man go across the yard, climb the stairs, and enter the house. He turned around then, to face Appleton.

"Marcus," he asked, "who do you expect to find?"

Appleton grinned at him. "Don't play dumb," he said. "You must know. Mona Campbell. You remember her."

"Yes. The woman in Timesearch. The one who disappeared."

Appleton nodded. "Boys down at the sector station spotted someone living here several weeks ago. When they flew over on a rescue mission. Then, a week or so ago, the same woman they had seen here came in, bringing a snakebit man. Said she'd found him on the road. Said she was just passing through. It was dark and they didn't get too good a look at her, but it was good enough. We put two and two together."

"You flunked out," Frost told him. "There has been no one here. No one here but me."

"Dan," said Appleton, "there's the matter of a murder charge that could be filed against you. If there's something you can tell us, we might forget we found you. Let you walk away."

"Walk how far?" asked Frost. "To decent bullet range, then get me in the back?"

Appleton shook his head. "A deal's a deal," he said. "We want you, of course, but the one we came looking for, the one we really want, is Mona Campbell."

"There's nothing to tell you, Marcus," said Frost. "If there were, I'd be tempted to pick up your deal—and bet with myself whether you would keep it. But Mona Campbell's not been here. I've never seen the woman."

Clarence came out of the house, walked heavy-footed to the gate.

"There's no one in there, Marcus," he said. "No sign of anyone."

"Well, now," said Appleton, "she must be hiding somewhere."

"Not in the house," said Clarence.

"Would you say," asked Appleton, "that this gentleman might know?"

Clarence swung his head around and squinted hard at Frost.

"He might," said Clarence. "There's just a chance he might."

"Trouble is," said Appleton, "he's not of a mind to talk."

Clarence swung a beefy hand, so fast there was no time to duck. It caught Frost across the face and drove him

backward. He struck the fence and slumped. Clarence
stooped and grasped his shirt and lifted him and swung the
hand again.

Brightly colored pinwheels exploded inside Frost's head
and he found himself crawling on his hands and knees,
shaking his head to get rid of the flaming pinwheels. Blood
was dribbling from his nose and there was a salt taste in his
mouth.

The hand reached down and lifted him again and set him
on his feet. Swaying, he fought to stay erect.

"Not again," Appleton said to Clarence. "Not right away,
at least. Maybe now he'll talk."

He said to Frost, "You want some more of it?"

"The hell with you," said Frost.

The hand struck again and he was down once more and
he wondered vaguely, as he tried to regain his feet, why
he'd said exactly what he had. It had been a dumb thing to
say. He'd not intended to say it and then he'd said it, and
look at what it got him.

He crawled to a sitting position and looked at the two
men. Appleton had lost his look of easy amusement. Clarence stood poised and watching him.

Frost put up a hand and wiped his face. It came away
smeared with dust and blood.

"It's easy, Dan," Appleton said to him. "All you have to
do is tell us where Mona Campbell is. Then you can walk
away. We haven't even seen you."

Frost shook his head.

"If you don't," said Appleton, "Clarence here will beat
you to death. He likes that kind of work and it might take
quite a little while. And the thought strikes me that the
boys from the sector station might not arrive in time. You
know that sometimes happens. They're just a little late and
it's too bad, of course, but there isn't much that can be done
about it."

Clarence moved a step closer.

"I mean it, Dan," said Appleton. "Don't think I am fooling."

Frost struggled to get his feet beneath him, poised to rise.
Clarence took another step toward him and started to reach
down. Frost launched himself at the two treelike legs in

front of him, felt his shoulder smash into them and sprawled flat upon his face. He rolled away blindly and got his feet beneath him and straightened.

Clarence was stretched upon the ground. Blood flowed across his face from a gash upon his head, apparently inflicted when, falling, he had struck a fence post.

Appleton was charging at him, head lowered. Frost tried to step away, but the man's head hit him and he fell, with Appleton on top of him. A hand caught his throat in a brutal grip and above his he saw the face, the narrowed eyes, the great gash of snarling teeth.

From far off, it seemed, he heard a thunder in the sky. But there was a roaring in his head and he could not be sure. The hand upon his throat had a viselike grip. He lifted a fist and struck at the face, but there was little power behind his blow. He struck again and yet again, but the hand upon his throat stayed and kept on squeezing.

A wind that came out of nowhere swirled dust and tiny pebbles through the air and he saw the face above him flinching in the dust. Then the hand at his throat fell away and the face swam out of sight.

Frost staggered to his feet.

Just beyond the car sat a helicopter, its rotors slowing to a halt. Two men were tumbling from the cabin and each of them had guns. They hit the ground and squared off, with the rifles at their hips. Off to one side, Frost saw Marcus Appleton, standing with his hands hanging at his side. Clarence still lay upon the ground.

The rotors came to a stop and there was a silence. Across the body of the cabin was the legend: RESCUE SERVICE.

One of the men made a motion with his gun at Marcus Appleton.

"Mr. Appleton," he said, "if you have a gun, throw it on the ground. You are under arrest."

"I have no gun," said Appleton. "I never carry one."

It was a dream, thought Frost. It had to be a dream. It was too fantastic and absurd not to be a dream.

"By whose authority," asked Appleton, "are you arresting me?"

There was mockery in his voice and he did not believe it. You could see that he did not believe it. No one, absolutely no one, could arrest Marcus Appleton.

"Marcus," said another voice, "it is on my authority."

Frost spun around and there, on the steps that led down from the cabin of the helicopter, was B.J.

"B.J.," said Appleton, "aren't you fairly far from home?"

B.J. didn't answer. He turned toward Frost. "How are you, Dan?" he asked.

Frost put up a hand and wiped his face. "I'm all right," he said. "Nice to see you, B.J."

The second man with a gun had gone over to Clarence and got him on his feet and relieved him of his gun. Clarence stood groggily, hand up to the gash upon his head.

B.J. had reached the ground and was walking out from the helicopter and Ann Harrison was coming down the steps.

Frost started toward the craft. His head was fuzzy and he could not feel his legs and was surprised that he could walk. But he was walking and he was all right and there was nothing that made sense.

"Ann," he asked, "Ann, what is going on?"

She stopped in front of him.

"What have they done to you?" she asked.

"Nothing that really amounted to anything," he said, "although they had a good start on it. But, tell me, what is this about?"

"The paper that you had. You remember, don't you?"

"Yes. I gave it to you that night. Or I thought I did. Was it really in that envelope?"

She nodded. "It was a silly thing. It said: 'Place 2468934' —isn't it ridiculous that I recall the numeral—'Place 2468934 on the list.' Do you remember now? You said you'd read it, but forgotten."

"I remember now it was about putting something on a list. What does it mean?"

"The numeral," said B.J., standing at his elbow, "is the designation of a person in the vaults. The list was a secret list of people who would never be revived. All record of them was to be wiped out. They would have disappeared from the human race."

"Not revived! But why?"

"They had substantial funds," said B.J. "Funds that could be channeled off. Channeled off and the records changed so

185

that the funds would not be missed if their owners were not revived and did not appear to claim them."

"Lane!" said Frost.

"Yes, Lane. The treasurer. He could manipulate such things. Marcus ferreted out the victims—those who had no close relatives, no close friends. People who would not be missed if they were not revived."

"You know, of course, B.J.," said Appleton, conversationally, without a trace of rancor in his voice, "that I will sue you for this. I'll make you a pauper. I'll take everything you have. You have committed this slander in front of witnesses."

"I doubt it very much," B.J. told him. "We have Lane's confession."

He nodded to the two men from the station. "Take them in," he said.

The two men began hustling Clarence and Appleton up the steps.

B.J. said to Frost, "You'll be coming back with us?"

Frost hesitated. "Why, I don't know . . ."

"The marks can be removed," said B.J. "There'll be an official announcement that will give you full credit for all that you have done. Your job is waiting for you. We have evidence that the trial and sentence was irregular and arranged by Marcus. And I would presume that Forever Center may find a means to show, in somewhat substantial manner, its gratitude for the interception of the paper . . ."

"But I didn't intercept it."

"Now, now," said B.J., reprovingly, "don't try to quibble with me. Miss Harrison informed us fully. She was the one who brought it to us, with the proof of what it was. Forever owes the two of you a debt it never can repay."

He turned abruptly and walked toward the helicopter.

"It was not really me," said Ann, "although I can't tell him who it was. It was George Sutton. He was the one who figured it all out, who ran it down and got the facts."

"Wait a minute, there," said Frost. "George Sutton? I don't know . . ."

"Yes, you do," she said. "The man who took you off the street that night. The Holy. The old gentleman who asked you if you believed in God."

"Dan!" B.J. had turned back toward them when he reached the foot of the stairs leading to the cabin.

"Yes, B.J."

"Marcus came out here hunting Mona Campbell. Said he had good evidence he would find her out here. Said an old farmhouse. I imagine it might have been this one."

"That is what he told me," Frost said evenly. "He seemed to think that I knew about her."

"And did you?"

Frost shook his head. "Not a thing," he said.

"Well," said B.J., "another wild goose chase. One of these days we'll catch up with her."

He went heavily up the steps.

"Just think," said Ann, "you'll be coming back. I can cook another dinner for you."

"And I," said Frost, "will go out and buy red roses and some candles."

He was remembering once again the warmth and comfort and the sense of life this woman could lend to a dowdy room—remembering, too, how the emptiness and bitterness of life had faded in her presence and how there had been companionship and friendliness such as he'd never known before.

Love? he wondered. Was this love? How was a man to know? In this first life that man lived there was scarcely time for love—nor the time, perhaps, to find out what it was. And would there be time in the second life? Time, surely, for there'd be all the time there was, but would one carry over into that infinitude of time the same sense of economic desperation, the same bleak materialism as he had held in the first life that he lived? Would he be a different man or the same as he had been—would the first life have set the pattern for all life yet to come?

She had turned her face to him and he saw her cheek was wet with tears. "It will be the same," she said.

"Yes," he promised. "It will be the same."

Although, he knew, it could not be the same. The earth would never be quite the same again. Mona Campbell had found a truth that she might never speak, but in a few years more there would be others who would find it and then the world would know. And once again the world would know the agony of conscience. Then the old solid certainty and the smug complacency would be riddled and Forever Center would have a rival in its promise—and this other promise would be one of mystery and faith, and once again the world of men would be ground between the millstones of opinion.

"Dan," said Ann, "please kiss me and then let us get aboard. B.J. will wonder what has happened to us."

37

THE man sat beside the road and stared into distance, but his eyes, one knew, saw nothing, and yet they were not empty eyes.

He wore only a pair of trousers, cut off well above the knees. His hair was long and hung down about his face. His beard was tangled and was full of sand. He was gaunt and his skin burned black by the sun.

Mona Campbell stopped her car and got out of it and stood, for a moment, watching him. There was no sign that he was aware of her and her heart welled up with pity at the sight of him, for there was about him a lostness and an emptiness that robbed existence of all meaning.

"Is there anything," she asked, "that I can do for you?"

His eyes changed at the sound of her voice. His head moved slightly and the eyes stared out at her.

"What is wrong?" she asked.

"What is wrong?" he asked, his voice rising sharply on the question. "What is right? Can you tell what's wrong or right?"

"Sometimes," she said. "Not always. The line is often fine."

"If I had stayed," he said. "If I had prayed a little harder. If I had dug the deep hole and put up the cross. But it was no use . . ."

His voice trailed off into nothingness and his eyes once again stared off into a distance where there was nothing one might see.

She noticed then, for the first time, the sack that lay on the ground beside him, apparently made out of material he'd ripped off his trouser legs. It lay half open and inside it she saw the jumbled figures of the carven jade.

189

"Are you hungry?" she asked. "Are you ill? You're quite sure there's nothing I can do?"

It was insane, she thought, that she should have stopped, that she should be standing in this road talking to this lost and empty man.

He stirred slightly. His lips began to open, as if he meant to speak, then pressed tight again.

"If there's nothing I can do," she said, "I'll be moving on."

She turned back to the car.

"Wait," he said.

She turned back.

The stricken eyes were staring at her.

"Tell me," asked the man, "is there such a thing as truth?"

It was not an idle question. She sensed that it was not.

"I think there is," she said. "There's truth in mathematics."

"I asked for truth," he said, "and all I got were these."

His foot thrust out and kicked the bag. The jade lay scattered on the grass.

"Is that the way it always is?" he asked. "You hunt for truth and you get a booby prize. You find something that is not the truth, but take it because it is better than finding nothing."

She backed away. The man was plainly mad.

"That jade," she said. "There was another man who was hunting for the jade."

"You don't understand," he said.

She shook her head, anxious to be off.

"You said there was truth in mathematics. Is God a page of math?"

"I wouldn't know," she said. "I only stopped to see if I could help you."

"You can't," he said. "You can't help yourself. We had it once—that help of which all of us stand in need—and we lost it somewhere. There's no way to get it back. I know, because I tried."

"There may be a way," she told him softly. "There is an equation from a long forgotten planet . . ."

He half rose and his voice cracked and shrieked. "No

190

way, I tell you. No way! There was never more than one way and now it doesn't work."

She turned and fled. At the car she stopped and turned back toward him. He had slumped down again, but his eyes still stared at her, with a terrible horror in them.

She tried to speak, but the words clogged in her throat.

And across the space between them, he whispered at her, as if it may have been a secret that he meant to tell her.

"We have been abandoned," the ghastly whisper said. "God has turned His back on us."

SCIENCE FICTION AND FANTASY
FROM AVON ◬ BOOKS